"Quick! Get in," Rainey urged.

She pulled back the sheet, and Quinn slid in next to her. At first they pursued their enjoyment in silence; then she sighed. "It's luscious."

"Hmmm!" Quinn licked his lips. "Good!"

"So good."

"Oh, yes," he said. "Yes."

"So . . . so . . . wonn-derful, yes."

"Yes. Yes. Yes."

"Hmm-mm!" she said breathlessly.

"Hmm-mm!" he answered with a groan.

"Oh, Quinn! That was delicious." She closed her eyes and collapsed among the pillows.

"I'm glad it was good for you, too," he said. She could hear his spoon scraping the bottom of the ice cream carton.

Frances Davies was destined to be a writer. As she puts it: "I did not start writing until a month before I was born. 'Stop with the pickles!' I thrummed on the placental membrane. 'Send chocolate!'" She was also destined to have an outrageous sense of humor. It's not surprising, then, that *The Lady Is a Champ* comprises seasoned writing skills and sparkling wit. The result is total delight! Harlequin is fortunate to be able to welcome Frances into the fold, and we look forward to publishing many more first-rate Temptations by this exceptional Wisconsin writer.

The Lady Is a Champ

FRANCES DAVIES

Harlequin Books

TORONTO • NEW YORK • LONDON
AMSTERDAM • PARIS • SYDNEY • HAMBURG
STOCKHOLM • ATHENS • TOKYO • MILAN

To
Stove

Published January 1988

ISBN 0-373-25285-4

1

"OKAY, YOU WISE GUYS..." Rainey took a deep breath and punched her voice out over the Sports department as though it were a volleyball. "Who pinched my cheese Danish?"

Jellicoe chuckled, Billings snickered. The other sportswriters tapped at their keyboards with enraptured attention. Only Cal Cuddy looked up shaking his head and smiling. His unfailing kindness made her feel terrible, because she wanted his job.

"A joke's a joke, fellas," Rainey pleaded. "C'mon, guys, have a heart, I'm starving." Her plea was met by the muffled cacophony that was as close to silence as the Sports department ever came.

"Thieves, that's what you are, a bunch of crummy thieves." She glared at Billings, just in case.

"Archer. *Rai*-ney *Arr-chur!*" her name came booming back, a redoubled baritone echo that rolled like a thunder clap. It was Wolfe, her editor.

She threw Jellicoe a disgusted look as she sprinted toward Wolfe's desk. With her eyes squinched to slits so that she could put the Evil Eye on the back of Billings's head, she collided with Quinn in front of the elevators. He caught her in his arms.

"Easy there, Champ." Quinn's black eyes glittered as he grinned down at her. "You okay?" He gave her a more than friendly squeeze.

"Murmff," she said, her mouth still pressed against his shirt.

Quinn released his grip, but only to step back and hold her by the elbows. Smiling, he said, "I have to tell you, you were really great last night. I don't know another woman who would have done the things you did for me. Really, you were sensational. I haven't slept that well in months."

Jellicoe guffawed. Billings snickered.

"Now look, Quinn," said Rainey. She shook herself free. "Just because I...I mean, one night doesn't—"

The elevator doors sighed open. "See you tonight," said Quinn, backing into the elevator. He grinned as the doors closed.

"*Archer!*" boomed Wolfe. "Where the hell are you?"

She hurried to his desk.

Wolfe said, "That was a first-rate piece of work you did in Bloomington."

"Well...thanks," she said, dumbfounded. Wolfe handed out compliments about once a century. He was compact and swarthy, a strong, wiry man who had once dreamed of playing professional ice hockey after college.

"Don't tell me," she said, "I can guess. You liked my stories so much you're going to let me do a piece on the Yankees. We're playing at home today, you know."

Wolfe shook his head gloomily. "I know."

"And here I thought I was wearing you down. Wolfe, you have a heart like a hockey puck."

Wolfe closed his eyes and sighed heavily.

"The Mets?" she said. "I'd settle for the Mets."

"Not yet."

From her first day at the *New York Journal* she had chipped away at Wolfe's stubborn reluctance to assign her to a baseball story. They both knew she was good enough, but for some reason he couldn't seem to bring himself to make the assignment, however determined she might be. After three years they were at a Mexican standoff. He said, When you're ready. She said, I'm ready now. He replied, Not yet. She thought her chance had come in early June, when Bud Morrow, the *Journal's* baseball writer, fell down a manhole across from Doyle's bar and broke both ankles. Wolfe gave Morrow's assignments to Cal Cuddy. On the day the ambulance brought Morrow home from the hospital, Rainey took him her chipped-beef and cottage cheese casserole and a quart of scotch in the hope he would put in a word for her. But July was almost over and Cuddy kept the cherished baseball beat, while Morrow hinted for another quart.

Wolfe said, "We're putting together a piece for tomorrow on how our local runners are training for the New York marathon in October. I've got a couple of sidebar stories for you. When you were in Indiana yesterday, Jack Becker was run down by a cyclist in Central Park and tore his Achilles tendon."

Rainey winced. "That's awful!"

"Yeah. He's over at New York Orthopedic. Go find out if he's going to be able to run again. And if so when. I can't believe he'll be ready for the marathon, so give me a real heart-tugging, RUNNER'S HOPES DASHED story. Then catch Monica Allen-Harte. She's pregnant and still training."

"I hadn't heard that."

"It must have happened just before the Boston Marathon. So find out how she's doing, what her doctor says, all that stuff. And take a good look and see if she shows. If she shows, I'll send someone out for a picture and we'll do a follow-up." She got up to leave, but Wolfe said, "How was that new photographer, what's his name. . . ."

"Quinn."

"Yeah, Quinn. How was he to work with? His pix are great."

"Fine," she said in her most noncommittal voice. "He was fine."

"You may be seeing a lot of him. Fontinella won't be back on the job for a month."

She headed for the elevator and the coffee shop around the corner. Even Wolfe couldn't expect her to interview Jack Becker on an empty stomach, and she needed to grab a few minutes to herself so that she could think about Quinn.

"The cheese Danish is gone already," said the waiter. "Try the poppy-seed."

Eating poppy seeds was like eating dust. "How about prune?" she suggested.

The waiter shook his head, an infinity of resignation in his eyes. "You should try the poppy-seed."

"But I'd rather have prune."

"The prune is gone already."

"Right," she said. "Poppy-seed." Why did she feel as though she'd just gone ten rounds with a crafty bantamweight?

She sipped her coffee and thought about Quinn who had very nearly missed the NCAA swimming meet at Indiana University. Was it only yesterday afternoon? It felt like a month ago. It had been the last day of the competition, and she'd been brooding over her lunch. She calculated that if the water from all the pools of all the swimming meets she had ever covered were added to all the pools that waited, lapping gently, in her future, there would be enough to irrigate the entire Southwest until the year 2055. How could she ever hope to write the Perfect Exclusive every reporter dreamed of, the story that would knock Wolfe's socks off, when he stuck her with every swimming assignment that came across his desk.

She stared malevolently into her water glass and vowed never to touch another drop of the stuff. A shadow fell across the table. She looked up and up and up, and there he was, looming over her like a pine tree.

"Archer?" he said, scanning her press badge for confirmation. "I'm Quinn."

She looked up into the rugged sun-bronzed face and immediately thought of the white-hatted Good Guy who fearlessly rode in the lead of the sheriff's posse. "Howdy?" she said, suppressing a grin. Quinn was a ringer for the rancher who bravely left his spread, muttering, "I gotta go, Mae. Someone's gotta help the sheriff rid the valley of them thievin' rustlers." He wore a khaki shirt, open at the throat and tucked into faded jeans slung low on his hips, and Nike climbing boots.

"I'm Quinn," he said again, as though he expected her to recognize the name. "I'm your new photographer."

"What did you do, ride into town on a slew-footed mule? You're two days late. That's two whole days I've had to take my own pictures. And I am not a picture person, Quinn. I am a word person. Taking pictures gives me a headache." He extended his hand, but she couldn't take it. She had both of hers wrapped around a Giant Hoosier Burger the size of a Frisbee. She nodded at the chair across from her, but he was already folding himself into it. Six foot four, she guessed, and training-peak lean. Was it the light she wondered that made his eyes seem so unnaturally large and black?

"What did you do with your last photog?" he said cheerfully. "Throw him in the pool, or eat him alive?"

"You're a real wit, Quinn. As it happens *she*—" she came down heavily on the she "—is in the Bloomington Hospital having her appendix out even as we speak. You were supposed to be here forty-eight hours ago."

"So you said." Were his eyes twinkling at her?

"You missed the water polo," she said sternly.

"Aw shucks!" He grinned and rubbed his chin.

"The only event left is the diving final this afternoon. Where have you been fooling around all this time? I need someone I can count on in relief."

"Have you any idea how long it takes to get to Bloomington, Indiana, from the Peruvian Andes?" He looked at her plate. "How are the burgers?"

"Fine. You were supposed to fly, not come by yak. What were you doing in the Andes?"

"Shooting the ruins at Macha Picchu. The *Journal* didn't wire me that I was hired until two days ago. And it's llamas in Peru, not yaks. Yaks are in Tibet." He ordered two Giant Hoosier Burgers, extra cheese, hold the bacon, hold the mayo, and two bottles of St. Pauli Girl. "I was promised a slot on a Foreign desk, but there's been some screw-up, so they've stuck me in Sports until a slot opens up. I'm not sure what the hitch is, but I'll have to wait it out."

"Gee, that's too bad, Quinn. My heart bleeds for you." She figured there were probably nine hundred young photographers in America who would do anything to get the job they'd handed Quinn. "What have you got against the Sports department? What's so great about a Foreign desk? Are you one of those macho guys whose adrenaline is so slow it doesn't pump unless they're in danger and frightened half out of their wits?"

He spread his big hands on the table and leaned toward her, supporting himself on his fingertips, and she noticed how far his thumbs flexed back at the first joint. "That's a liar's thumb," her mother used to say. "Your father's thumbs did that."

"Money," said Quinn cheerfully. "Money, pure and simple. I'm behind in my alimony. The Foreign desk pays more than Sports. Didn't you know that?" He squirted catsup on his burgers, chewed a thoughtful bite and washed it down with beer. "No cheeseburgers in Peru. That's the thing I miss most when I'm overseas. There's nothing in the world a man could want that he can't find on foreign soil—except real cheeseburgers." He took another bite and rolled his eyes. "Bliss," he said out of the corner of his mouth.

She reached for a last bite of her Danish, but discovered she'd finished it. Still hungry, she took the subway uptown to interview Jack Becker. She knew her HEELLESS RUNNER interview would be a good one because she got the last seat in her car, and she believed in omens, sometimes.

Finding one of Quinn's pictures in a magazine on the plane that night—that had to have been an omen, though of what she was not at all sure. During the flight back from Bloomington she had been leafing idly through a dog-eared copy of *Travel and Leisure*, her heart swelling with pity for Micronesian Stone Age cultures where no one had ever heard of baseball, when she turned a page and came upon a stunning double-page spread of Mt. Kilimanjaro. M.A.

Quinn, read the credit line. A surreptitious glance at Quinn in the seat beside her caught him watching her out of the corner of his eye. He busied himself popping the top of a can of Heinekin and pretended not to notice his picture spread out on her lap. He had long, dexterous hands, she noticed not for the first time, lightly callused and corded with strong blue veins. She might overlook his thumbs.

Finally she relented and said, "This is yours, isn't it?"

"Hmm." He sipped his beer.

"It's gorgeous. It really is. I can understand why you might not be too thrilled to find yourself covering college diving after doing things like this. Why did you sign on with the *Journal*?"

"The bottom's fallen out of the exotic travel market, in case you hadn't heard. You could roll a bocci ball down the Via Veneto this year and never hit a tourist. The travel pix market will come back—eventually. And by the time it does I'll be caught up on my alimony." He tipped his head back to drain his beer. "I had to choose between accepting the *Journal*'s offer and marrying a rich Peruvian widow who could pay my alimony for me—"

"And being a clean-living boy you decided against the rich widow."

Quinn's eyes sparkled mischievously. "Are you by any chance a rich woman who'd pay my alimony in exchange for my beautiful manly body?"

"No," said Rainey, grinning in spite of herself. "I am not rich, and I'm not interested in your manly body."

"You shouldn't turn it down without trying it—it's been highly praised on seven continents and thirty-four islands." Somehow, his eyes had gathered in all the light—they glowed at her.

"Forget it, Quinn."

The intercom crackled with the sound of someone crumpling a wad of cellophane in her ear. The hair on the back of her neck stood up. Was this the best the airline could afford? If the intercom system was a UL reject, where did they shop for their cabin instruments? Toys-R-Us? And where did they find their pilots?

"Ev'nin all," drawled a middling tenor in earnest imitation of Chuck Yeager. Ever since *The Right Stuff*, all airline pilots sounded like America's heroic test pilot. Was the right drawl a prerequisite of employment? Maybe it was a class they taught in pilot's school. Pilot-Passenger Interactions: Talkin' Raht'll Make 'em Feel Real Comfy.

She hated flying. She had no fear of heights, snow had yet to fall on the ski slope she wouldn't attempt. No, it wasn't the altitude, it was the lack of control. Her life was in the hands of a man she'd never even met. What if he hated his job? Hated it so much he was filled with self-destructive impulses? She'd once been on a New York bus when the driver had pulled to the curb in front of Ralph Lauren's Polo Shop, turned to the startled passengers and shouted, "There is a life

above and a life below. I am joining the life below."
Then he stepped down into the street, heaved up a
manhole cover and disappeared down the manhole.
She followed, notebook in hand, anxious for his story.
But he had pulled the manhole cover back into place,
and she wasn't strong enough to raise it. DISAPPEAR-
ING DRIVER STRANDS BUS, her story was headed, but
she never found out why he'd chosen that moment to
slip away through Ralph Lauren's manhole. She took
the next bus.

But there was no next plane if your pilot was secretly seeking some manhole in the sky.

"An' owa flaht time," the pilot concluded, "will be
one owa twenty-two minutes. Y'all en-joy the flaht
now, y'hear?"

Sweat broke out on her upper lip.

"White-knuckle flyer?" said Quinn.

"Always have been," she admitted. "It's not being
up here that gets to me; it's not knowing what sort of
loony is at the controls."

"There's a sure cure for that," he said cheerfully. "I
could cure you myself, if you'd like."

She regarded him suspiciously. "How?"

"By teaching you to fly."

"Me? Fly? You must be out of your mind. If God
had wanted us to fly, he would have given us landing
gear."

"If you were the one at the controls it wouldn't
bother you. Believe me, I know." He tore open a
packet of Flite-nuts and offered them. She shook her

head. He studied her while he chewed. "Weren't you the little kid Ace Archer used to sneak into the Yankee dugout? Weren't you the one with the pigtails all the guys called Champ?"

"How do you know that?"

"I used to see your picture on the sports page, and on TV. When I was a teenager I thought you were the luckiest ten-year-old in the whole world. And the prettiest. I'm pleased to meet you, Champ." He grinned as he took her hand in his.

His palm was warm, very warm, but his fingertips were icy from holding the beer can. The contrast was almost erotic. It made her shiver.

He looked over at her from beneath lowered lashes. "I have to be honest with you, Champ. It really shakes me up that the pretty little kid with the yellow pigtails has turned into such a good-looking woman. I've never liked working with beautiful women. It makes me very uncomfortable." He shifted in his seat.

"Don't knock it till you've tried it, Quinn. Photographers on seven islands and thirty-four continents have been clamoring to work with me." Why did he have such wickedly enticing eyes and such impossibly thick and curly hair? If he had been bald with pale eyes, he would have been so easy to ignore. And why did he have that deep cleft in his chin? And why did it drive her so wild? His evening beard was beginning to show, and she knew if she bit his chin it would be prickly against her tongue.

She shifted in her seat and the magazine slid to the deck. They reached down for it in unison, their hands closing on it simultaneously, their faces cheek to cheek. In a flash Quinn kissed her, his lips like his hands both hot and cool. Her heart dropped a thousand feet.

"Not bad for a gringo," he said a moment later. "Why don't you hang up your spikes and come away with me? I'll take you to Cuzco and make love to you Peruvian style."

Rainey laughed to cover her confusion. Why was she so breathless? Would the plane stop if she grabbed for the oxygen mask? No, that was trains. "Aren't you forgetting about your alimony?" she managed finally.

"Yeah," he said glumly. "Are you sure you're not rich?"

"Don't worry, Quinn, Manhattan is crammed with rich and lusty widows."

He hunched his shoulders and groaned with despair. "But not with your biteable tush."

She had hidden her blazing face behind Mt. Kilimanjaro, but a day later her lips still tingled with the memory of that kiss. What is it about Quinn? she wondered as her train clattered into the station. She climbed the stairs to the street asking herself, why do I care, and why can't I get the man out of my head?

Looking back on it now, she did feel as though she'd known Quinn for weeks and weeks, knew him far better than she wanted to.

THE HOSPITAL RECEPTIONIST, who looked like the guard of cell block seven in *Women Behind Bars*, squinted at her suspiciously. "Mr. Becker is not seeing anyone, I'm sorry. You're not from the press are you?"

"Oh, no!" Rainey smiled sweetly. She took off her sunglasses with a gesture that had sincerity written all over it. "Jack and I are old friends. We both train with the New York Road Runners."

"*Sports Illustrated* was here ten minutes ago," said the guard. "I threw them out." She glowed with triumph.

"They're such a nuisance," Rainey agreed. "Could you give me Jack's room number? I'd like to send him some wheat grass and bee pollen."

"You runners!" she said in disgust. "You'll eat anything."

Rainey grinned weakly and tried for a self-deprecating smile.

"Mr. Becker's in 1428 West."

"Thanks," said Rainey, leaning across the reception desk to whisper, "Could I use the ladies' room before I leave?"

"Sure, honey. It's just down that hall, second door on the left."

Rainey closed the ladies' room door, counted slowly to twenty, opened the door and walked quickly down the length of the corridor and into a waiting elevator.

"Jack," she called a few minutes later, peering around the door of room 1428 West. "What happened?"

"Rainey! How did you get in here?" A scowling Jack Becker lay flat on his back, one plaster-encased leg suspended from the ceiling.

"I lied."

Jack burst out laughing. "Rainey, you're the only good thing that's happened to me since I've been in here. Come on in and shut that door."

Rainey took out her notebook. "How did it happen?"

"I should have seen him coming," he said. "He blindsided me."

She was still thinking of Jack's words as she scrambled aboard a train to her next interview. *Jack's not the only one,* she said to herself. *I should have seen Quinn coming. Should have seen . . . should have seen . . . should have seen Quinn coming.* Her thoughts matched the rhythm of the subway train that was carrying her to RUNNING MOM. Was it, she wondered, because Quinn was so smooth that she didn't see through from the beginning? Could anyone else have predicted what Quinn would do when they got off the plane?

"Can I get your bag for you?" Quinn had said eagerly, the moment the wheels bumped down at LaGuardia. "How about your computer? Could I carry your computer?"

"It's a portable, Quinn, only ten pounds." She tried not to grin. Why was he suddenly all over her like a blanket? But blanket made her think of bed, and bed made her wonder what Quinn would be like in it, and then she stumbled stepping off the escalator to the baggage claim, and Quinn caught her from behind, his arm around her waist.

"Easy there, Champ," he said, his lips close to her ear.

Her heart dropped another thousand feet. When would it hit ground?

"Share a cab?" offered Quinn as they headed for the cab rank outside the terminal.

"Where are you going?" asked Rainey. "I live on the west side."

"The thing is…" he began. His eyes, avoiding hers, focused about three inches to the right of her right ear. "I don't have a place lined up yet. I've been overseas so long I don't know anyone in New York well enough to ask them to put me up, and—" He dug his hands into his trouser pockets and stared at his toe caps.

"Why don't you stay at a hotel?" she said.

"I spent my last buck getting to Bloomington."

"The Y?"

At last his eyes found hers. They were glowing again. He took a deep breath. "Could I stay at your place?"

"I don't have any room."

"Just for one night. Two at the most. I'm sure the *Journal* will give me a draw against my salary."

"I don't have anything for you to sleep on. There's nothing but an old sofa in the living room, and that's all sprung—"

"Just until I can find a place—"

"You could be crippled for life, sleeping on that thing—"

"Sofa springs don't matter to me, Champ. I'm young, I'm strong, I'm healthy. I've slept on the floor of a yurt with a snoring goat for a pillow."

"It's impossible. I've never shared with anyone, much less a...a...well, I've never shared. I'm a very private person with a teeny, weeny apartment. It's out of the question."

"Just until I get some cash together and find a place—"

"No!" she said, stepping into a cab. Quinn slid in beside her.

"Where to, buddy?" said the driver.

"How about the Salvation Army?" said Quinn.

2

"IT'S ONLY FAIR to warn you," she said to Quinn as she paid the cabdriver, "this is not the greatest neighborhood in New York. I mean I was mugged at high noon on my way back from Zabar's."

He held the street door for her. "You were hurt?"

"My pride was mighty sore, I can tell you. He shoved me into a snow bank and got away with my watch, a pound of lox and a quart of Häagen-Dazs rum-raisin. I went out the next day and signed up for a karate course."

She started up the stairs. "And there's no elevator, Quinn. Wouldn't you rather stay with someone on the east side? It's safer on the east side. Everyone on the east side has an elevator."

"I don't know anyone on the east side," said Quinn.

"And they never have dust mice. Just look at that." She pointed to a tangled nest of dust on the landing. "Dino, our super, cultivates them. He's got this special compound he sprinkles on the steps to make them grow. He's saving them to stuff a mattress." Quinn showed no sign of retreat. She dug into the bottom of her purse for her keys. "Would it make any difference to you if I told you the guy across the hall keeps a python?"

"Let me get that door for you," said Quinn.

With some little effort Rainey had succeeded in persuading herself that her apartment was not cramped, but cozy. "It's sort of snuggled under the eaves of an old brownstone," she would say cheerfully, adding, "It's cozy. No wasted space," or "Fits me like a batting glove, ha, ha." But now, with Quinn standing in the middle of her living room, with his arms upraised—he was fingering her favorite ceiling crack: the one that looked like Yogi Berra—the place seemed about as spacious as Snoopy's doghouse.

"Hey," said Quinn, running his finger over Yogi's nose. "Look at this. It looks just like Mt. Whitney."

Rainey threw open a window. All the soot on Eighty-first Street blew in. She closed the window and turned on the air conditioner.

"One of these days," she began lamely, "I'm going to give this place a good going over . . . I've been meaning to fix it up, I really hate the doggy-brown wallpaper, but somehow . . . well, you know how it is, I never seem to get around to it. . . ." She watched him taking in her crammed and dusty bookcases, the lumpy stuffed chairs and sofa, the scattering of tape cassettes on the coffee table.

In three strides Quinn crossed the living room to the kitchen with its minuscule stove and wheezing refrigerator. Her narrow teak table and two chairs were pushed against the window to catch the morning sun. On a clear day she could see West End Avenue.

"Your kitchen's about as big as a howdah," said Quinn with a chuckle. He looked about nine feet tall leaning against the fridge. "But it's got . . . um, possibilities," he finished ambiguously.

"A howdah?"

"The little covered seat, it's sort of like a box—" he shaped a box with his hands "—it's where you sit when you ride an elephant."

"It is? I thought that was a . . ." What was the word? The ceiling light made Quinn's eyes glitter when he smiled and the glitter blew great gaps in her concentration. "Mahout," she said, finally. "I thought the box on an elephant was a mahout."

"The mahout's the guy who sits behind the elephant's head; he's the elephant driver." The light picked out a sheen of deep red highlights in his black hair.

"Sure. I knew that. I just forgot." Why was he smiling at her like that? Didn't he believe her? He had the most perfect uncapped teeth she'd ever seen. Strong, but not too big, and milky white. Smooth. Glistening. Slick. "How . . . ?" she began, but her voice was so high she swallowed and tried again. "How does he keep from falling off? The mahout."

Quinn rested his big warm hands on her shoulders and his eyes went straight into hers and did a little dance against the back of her skull. His thumbs pressed lightly on the wings of her collarbone, and all her ribs buzzed.

"Thighs," he said, his voice rumbling up from some wizard's cave deep in his chest. "They know how to grip with their thighs."

"I should have guessed," she sputtered, ducking out from beneath his thumbs. She turned back into the living room. "You can see how small this place is. And that couch. I mean as a place to sleep it's really the pits, and—"

"It'll be fine," Quinn insisted. "Don't worry about me."

Resigned, she said, "If you'll follow me, I'll show you where the bathroom is. I'm sure you must want a towel. Let me get you a towel." She fled to the cupboard across from the bathroom. "I hope you don't have a color preference, because all I have is yellow. I like yellow. Do you like yellow? Here, take two towels. And a washcloth. And a couple of sheets for the sofa, and a pillow."

He rested his chin on the pile of linen in his arms and smiled inscrutably.

"And this—" She pushed open the door. "This is the john. If the shower water comes out all rusty, just let it run, it'll go away in a couple minutes.... And, um..." But she had run down and couldn't think what to say next.

"And that?" Quinn nodded at the closed door adjacent to the bathroom.

"That's my bedroom." Her bedroom was absolutely, positively out of bounds. If he so much as asked to see it, she'd show him one of Wada-san's karate moves.

"Right," he said, turning back to the living room. "Where can I hang my clothes?" He dropped the linen on the sofa.

"Hang your clothes? Why do you want to hang your clothes? You'll be gone in eight hours. I mean you're sure to find an apartment tomorrow. You can look before work—we start at ten o'clock. Did they tell you that? And you can look on your lunch hour, and again after work. I know you're going to find a place tomorrow."

"I don't want to impose on your hospitality, but I'm an ex-Navy man, and I like to keep a crease in my jeans."

"The front closet," she said weakly. "Next to the front door. Just give my coats a shove."

He opened the closet door. "Where would you like me to put your bicycle?"

"Bicycle? Oh, yeah. Right here, I guess, next to the bookcase." She couldn't very well stand there watching him unpack his duffel bag, so she said, "I guess I'll have a shower and turn in. It's been a long day."

"Right," he said cheerfully. "I'll shower in the morning."

She twirled the taps and bleakly watched the rusty water swirling down the drain while she waited for the hot water to come up. *What could I have done?* she asked herself as she shampooed her hair. *What alternatives do I have?* She couldn't tell him to go sleep with the winos at the Salvation Army. She couldn't ask him to bed down with druggies and crazies. He was a fellow journalist, after all. . . .

She pulled on her robe and opened the door. "Uh, good night," she called as she dashed from the bathroom to her bedroom.

"Sleep warm," he called from the sofa.

She closed her bedroom door, turned the air conditioner up to Igloo, pulled the phone into bed with her and dialed Mo, pulling the blanket over her head to muffle her voice. She let the phone ring. Mo never picked up until after a zillion rings.

"Mo?" she whispered.

"Rainey?" said Mo. "Why are you whispering?"

"I don't want him to hear me."

"Oh, my God! Are you being mugged again? Should I call the police? Are you hurt? What's going on?"

"I'm fine," whispered Rainey. "I'm not being mugged. I just wanted you to know—in case you called and a man answered—that I've got a guy staying here for a day or two."

"Is that all?" Mo let out a windy sigh. "Well it's about time. Who is he?"

"It's not like that, Mo. I only met him this afternoon in Indiana."

"Fast worker." Mo chuckled.

"If you're going to be snide, I won't tell you about him."

"If you don't tell me, I'll start spreading rumors on Madison Avenue that you're finally quitting the paper to join my agency. Then Wolfe will fire you, and I'll be able to put you to work writing ad copy for Pilson tennis racquets and Zap-Flite balls, and you can make us both rich."

"Don't you dare!" Mo had been her best friend since her sophomore year in high school. Everyone at St. Scholastica's knew Rainey wanted to be a sportswriter, but Rainey was the only one in the whole world who ever knew that Maureen Cunningham wanted to be a poet, like Sylvia Plath. At sixteen, she longed to live intensely, marry another poet, and die young, leaving her poems as a shining legacy to the generations to come. Today, she owned her own ad agency.

"Rainey," said Mo. "Something must be going on. You haven't called me at midnight to talk about a man since Mario quit the racing circuit and went back to Italy. And we both know how long ago that was."

"Yes," agreed Rainey ruefully. "Three years." Then she told Mo all about her meeting with Quinn. She meant to tell her just the circumstances, but somehow she found herself talking about his extraordinary eyes, and how thick and black his hair was, and how they'd both reached for her fallen magazine and he'd impulsively kissed her. And how damned nervous she felt having him right there in her living room, his long lean body stretched out on her sofa.

"I should be so lucky," said Mo.

"I don't suppose you know of a really cheap apartment for rent. Maybe a sublet?"

"I'll ask around," said Mo. "But if your Quinn were sleeping on my sofa, I'd lock the front door and throw the key out the window."

When she woke in the morning he had already left, leaving behind a pot of coffee and a plundered morning paper. He had taken the real estate section and the crossword. With any luck, she thought, he'd be out of there before she got back from work that night. It was going to be difficult enough working with him when he was assigned to her, but that wasn't up to her. She couldn't very well tell Wolfe or the photo editor that she preferred someone else.

RAINEY FOUND her RUNNING MOM eager to talk about the positive effects of her new hormone balance on her training, and how pleased her Ob-Gyn was with her all-round good health. The October marathon would be out, but she was hoping to win a 10K in Baltimore next Sunday. They sat over peanut butter sandwiches and lemonade in Monica's kitchen and talked 10K strategy and pregnancy and made corny jokes about running infants.

Rainey listened and made notes. The most important thing she had learned from reading Red Smith's sports columns all her life was that writing sports was really writing people. After an hour she headed back to the *Journal* to write her stories. Nasty Norman, the copy editor who usually took her stories was a bear about making the late-afternoon deadline.

When she handed Norman her summaries he scanned them, drained his coffee cup and goggled at her over the tops of his half glasses. "Archer," he said, "where was your head today?"

She stared at him. "What do you mean?"

"In your lead you call this guy Becker. In the rest of the summary you call him Quinn. Now which is it?"

"Becker," she said, mortified. "His name is Becker. Sorry, Norman, it must be the heat, or something. It's been a crazy day."

Norman threw her pages at her. "Rewrite this garbage."

SHE KNEW Quinn was in her apartment even before she put her key in the first lock. She didn't know how she knew, but she knew. She could feel it. It was almost as though some mysterious electrical charge leaked from his fingertips to crackle in the surrounding air. "Quinn?" she called cautiously. Perhaps he was packing.

But he was not packing. He sat at one end of the sofa tinkering with an eviscerated camera body.

"Did you find a place?" She tossed her jacket over her bike's now convenient handlebars and dropped into a chair. "Did you get your advance?"

He laid the camera carefully on the coffee table. "Hi!" he said, grinning.

"So, what happened?" she prompted.

"How about a beer?" He stretched languidly.

"I don't have any beer. In fact there isn't anything to eat. I thought I'd shop as soon as I can change into something cooler. It's getting very hot out there. Tomorrow some poor slob of a Metro reporter will be sent out to do yet another heat story. MERCURY SOARS. Boy, I'm glad I'm on sports. I don't think I could eat more than a salad. Or maybe some cold fruit. How about you?"

"I already shopped for you." He was halfway across the room and heading for the refrigerator.

"Then you did get your money. That's great. Did you find a place?"

He handed her a can of beer and a glass. "No. No I didn't. Do you have any idea how much they want for a security deposit these days? About equal to Canada's total defense budget."

"But what about your advance money?"

Quinn shrugged and looked down at his hands in the manner of a just man beleaguered. "I sent half of it to my wife's lawyer. I didn't have enough left for a security deposit even if I had found a place, which I didn't. I must have looked at six different places this morning and I wouldn't ask a camel driver to live in one of them." He picked up the camera and began reassembling it.

"C'mon, Quinn. Were you really trying?"

"I saw roaches this morning that you could throw a saddle on and ride in Central Park. How do people ever find habitable apartments in this city?" He peered at her through the viewfinder.

"Persistence. You have to keep looking. You should be out there pounding the streets right now."

"I'm giving it my best shot. Smile!"

She smiled into the lens. *Why, oh why,* she asked herself, *does he have to be so damned attractive? Why couldn't he be bald, or have arms covered with disgusting tattoos, or a face full of acne?*

"Great," he said, clicking off a shot. "What do you say we grab something to eat and go to a movie?" *Click.* "I haven't seen an American movie in three years. How about it?" *Click-click.* "I'll look at apartments again tomorrow. What did you do today?"

She couldn't very well say, "Mostly, I thought about you," so she said, "I did a couple of stories about runners. What about you?"

"I was out at Aqueduct shooting some great-looking horses." *Click.* "And a girl jockey who really knows how to use her thighs." *Click-click-click.*

RAINEY WATCHED the opening credits roll up on the screen and thought, Quinn is just a guy I work with. That he's staying at my place for a day or two is pure chance, and I ought to be able to handle that. After all, I'm a thirty-year-old mature woman. But if I'm so mature, why do I feel like a kid on her first date?

"Have some popcorn," whispered Quinn, holding the Biggie Bucket between them. He scrunched down on his tailbone and munched happily.

Quinn stretched as they came out of the theater, reaching wide with his arms and working his shoulders like a prize fighter with a crick in his neck. He hitched his jeans up and said, "Let's walk. I hate being cooped up in buses and subways."

It was a hot night, an easy night. The streetlamps were brightly haloed in the steamy, humid air. Everyone they passed was shiny with the heat, foreheads, noses, cheeks, chins, everyone shone as they walked or danced, loped, sashayed, jangled and jiggled, forming and reforming in patterns up and down Broadway and over on Columbus.

The air was filled with shouts and lovers' cries and fights and laughter, the distant wha-wha of sirens racing downtown. But tonight the music was all uptown. Music from chromed boxes shoulder-high, dudes bopping along beneath them, their eyes half-closed, their hips swiveling. Music poured down like cool water from bright windows higher still, and farthest up, in the pink mist-shrouded sky, the invisible stars made secret music for themselves.

Their journey back to her place was more a meander than a walk. They circled blocks, wandered from one side of the street to the other and back again. They found a sidewalk café where the air was pungent with the bitter-brown aroma of espresso, and there they sat and talked while up and down the street the lights in apartment houses winked out. Iron window grates rasped shut. Late shops went dark. The corner vegetable sellers hosed down their sidewalks and put up their clanging shutters.

An Afghan hound, dressed for safari in khaki fur, paced with delicate but determined steps from hydrant to hydrant, while the pale young man in khaki shorts who clung to his leash praised him extravagantly.

Quinn talked about his travels and how much it meant to him to be able to work as a free lance—beholden to no one, answerable to no one. He hated working for "the Man," as he put it. "A man should work for himself," he insisted. And once his alimony troubles were over—with his *Journal* job he expected to pay it all down in six months—he would be off again, heels flying.

"Who *was* that masked man?" she muttered to herself. "Why he's the Lone Ranger." She wondered if she was secretly longing to be rescued. From what? She studied his face, all angles and shadows in the yellow light beneath the café awning. His eyes were like pools of trust. And she was overcome by such a longing to talk to him that it frightened her half to death. She had never been able to talk with a man—not in the really intimate way she could talk with Mo. *What am I afraid of?* she asked herself. She didn't want to make any discoveries about herself—it was all she could do to cope with what she already knew. And she knew that if Quinn didn't find a place soon she was going to do something she would probably regret for a very long time.

"Quinn," she began, as they strolled up Columbus Avenue, "I think it's only fair that I tell you you'd better find a place tomorrow, or the day after at the latest, because I'm finding it very difficult having you around just now."

He didn't really touch her as they walked, but steered her with barely felt pressures—to her elbow, her shoulder, her arm—she felt like a perfectly handled skiff.

"Am I screwing up an ongoing romance? Who's the guy? Someone on the Sports desk?"

"No," she said. "It's not that. We're a lot alike, you and I. We both have plans, goals. Yours is to pay off your debts and get back to the bush, or the outback, or wherever. And nothing's going to interfere with that."

"Right," he said.

"Well, I have a plan, too. It's something I've dreamed of for years, and it takes all the energy I've got, because to get what I want I have to be two hundred percent better than any of the other sportswriters."

"It's not hard to guess, Champ. You want to cover baseball. Who's standing in your way? Wolfe?"

"I used to think that man was like a door without a handle. But I've been oiling his hinges. I've almost got him where I want him. He just needs a little nudge to push him open far enough for me to slip through. If he were a baseball fan I don't think I'd have to work so hard to convince him I really know my stuff—"

"You're Ace Archer's daughter. What more does he want?"

"That doesn't cut any ice with Wolfe. On my first day at the *Journal* he took me to lunch, and I made a damn fool of myself describing—in lurid detail—all the different elbow problems that sideline fork-ball pitchers. He couldn't have cared less. He's a hockey nut. If it isn't played on ice, forget it. But I think he's beginning to come around."

"I feel for you, Champ, but what has your plan got to do with me?"

"It doesn't have anything to do with you. That's just the point. I don't have any room in my life just now for anything but my work."

"You know what they say?" He grinned roguishly. "All work and no play—"

"I don't believe in that sort of play," she said firmly. "And I don't want to become the sort of woman who does. Who plays around." But if there was ever a man for whom she was in danger of throwing all her caveats out the window, that man was Quinn. And she didn't want to exhaust herself fighting him off on the one hand and battling her own physical desire on the other. She couldn't very well tell him that, so she said, "I need all my energy for my work."

"Sure," said Quinn. "Don't worry, I'll be out of your living room and out of your life by tomorrow night."

But he wasn't. He had looked at five apartments and found nothing. A few days later he had a lead on a loft sublet in the West Village, but the agency rep who had the key failed to keep his appointment, and she couldn't very well turn him out into the street, so she gave him a couple more days' grace. And suddenly two weeks had gone by and then three weeks, and still Quinn slept on her sofa.

At first she thought she wouldn't see much of Quinn. After all, she had her friends. But suddenly everyone she knew was either buried in work, like Mo, who was cooking up a new ad campaign, or out of the country, like Didi, who worked for *Time* and had gone to Brussels on assignment. Or simply out of the city, like Ellie, who had taken her kids to Ogunquit for the month. Then Beth and Johanna went to Austria to visit Caroline, and Alice took off for Greece. Suddenly, she and Quinn seemed to be the only ones left in New York. They might as well have been stranded on a desert island, she told herself.

They ate out more than they ate in—Quinn's passion for hamburgers never slackened. Twice she made her chipped-beef casserole, and he made Quinn Burgers: ground sirloin patties with pockets of hot, oozing Roquefort cheese inside, garnished with tomatoes, lettuce, raw mushrooms and sliced jalapeño peppers. After the first taste she threw out her recipe for tuna casserole.

On most nights they sat up late and talked. Once he spent an entire evening just talking about trees. He described pine forests in Germany, olive groves in Greece, umbrella pines in Italy, laurels in Japan, beechwoods in Hampshire and willows in France. Or he talked about Welsh valleys, or Austrian belfries, or Italian lakes, or the patterns of cobbled streets. And she told him about growing up in New York with a father who was practically a national hero. She told him stories of her first job on an upstate weekly where, like all freshman reporters, she had been condemned to cover hour after hour of mind-numbing sewer commission meetings. Sometimes they talked about movies, and sometimes they talked about books, but mostly, they talked about themselves.

It was at Yankee stadium, in the bottom of the seventh inning, with the Yankees losing to the Minnesota Twins, that Rainey finally asked Quinn the question that had been lurking like a black fish just below the surface of her mind.

"Quinn," she said, taking a deep breath. "Are you paying child support?"

He stared at her, his eyes wide with surprise. "No kids, no child support. Ex-wife, ex-wife support. Want another hot dog?"

"Sure. You must have done something pretty awful. You're the only divorced man I've ever met who's had to pay alimony."

"I never did a thing. Really. She just hated going to places like Sumatra and Borneo and living on rice and fish."

"What did she do before you married her?"

"The same thing she does now. She runs a cooking school in Chicago called, *C'est de bon goût*. The truth is, she's a very vindictive woman with a Sicilian idea of honor. So what do I draw but a woman judge named Cefalu. Angelina Cefalu. I was lucky to get out of that courtroom with my thumbs."

Some days she told herself Quinn was just a fellow worker, a buddy she was helping out—no more—and on some days she managed to believe it. But on the other days she found it harder and harder to concentrate on her assignments, because she kept remembering how Quinn closed his eyes when he listened to music, and how his dense black lashes made soft, purple shadows on his cheeks. Or she remembered how he never managed to get his back quite dry, and his fresh shirt clung to his back in little damp, transparent patches. She longed to say, "Take off your shirt, Quinn, and let me dry your back," but she bit her tongue. It was all too easy to imagine rubbing his bronzed back with a bright yellow towel, his muscles bunching beneath her fingers. These were the days when she knew she was kidding herself.

On those nights when she got back from the paper before he did, the place seemed so empty she found herself doing things so dumb she couldn't even explain them to herself—like walking into the bathroom to stare at his lumpy, blue nylon shaving kit. On impulse, she unzipped it and peeked inside. Then she locked the bathroom door and examined the contents. The razor was American, the blades English, but the label on the shaving foam was French. The convex metal shaving mirror that made her look like a pug-nosed fish could have come from anywhere.

The only word on the comb was Ace. The labels on his antiperspirant, toothbrush and paste were all in Spanish. At the very bottom she found a year-old bottle of antimalaria pills from a pharmacy in Nairobi, and ten packets of condoms from Buy-Rite Drugs around the corner. *Ten?* She counted them twice, put everything back and zipped the kit, her face burning.

On working days he was always gone when she got up, but he always left a note propped against the coffeepot. There were silly notes that made her smile:

"I dreamed last night of Kashmir and a houseboat on Lake Srinagar. Do you think that means I will meet my karma today, or that we should go out for a curry dinner?"

And practical notes that made her smile even more:

"Where did you hide the laundry ticket??? I'll pick up the laundry after work, if you'll bring the ticket to the office. Where is it? If you can't find it, *you'll* have to charm Chin Lee. Mr. Chin is immune to mine."

She knew it was foolish, but sometimes she carried his morning note around in her pocket all day to take out and reread as she traveled around the city. If she stared long enough at the black, reflecting window of the subway train, she saw Quinn's smile. In her wallet was an inch-square photo of the two of them clowning for the camera in a photo booth in Grand Central Station. Wearing Yankee caps, their heads together to squeeze into the frame, both a little tipsy after clams and beer in the Oyster Bar, they grinned into the lens. When she saw the print she thought, *We look like lovers.*

On Saturday mornings, he'd rap on her bedroom door calling, "Roll out, Champ! We're going to swab the decks." She vacuumed, Quinn mopped, washed the windows and chewed her out like a bos'n if she left any dust in the corners. Then they'd take sandwiches to the park and spend the day baking in the sun, listening to her jazz tapes, reading and talking about everything and nothing.

"Did you always want to be a photographer?" she asked. "Did you get a camera for Christmas when you were eight and fall in love with pictures?" It was easy to imagine Quinn as an intensely serious, camera-mad boy. The kind of kid who would build a darkroom in his closet and cover his bedroom walls with sour-smelling prints.

Quinn closed his book and rolled on his side. He propped his head on his hand. "Not that young. I went with my sixth-grade class to see a show of Ansel Adams's pictures of the High Sierras. He amazed me. He astonished me. The power, the drama, the heart-stunning beauty of his images—his pictures hit me like a tremendous blow, like grace." He tugged at a tuft of grass. "Do you know what I mean?"

"I think so," she said.

"From that day on, I was hooked. I haunted the Art Institute, cut classes to take pictures of Lake Michigan.... I was big on raging storms, in those days—the wilder the better. And what about you? What made you decide to be a baseball writer and not...oh, I don't know... a professional tennis player, or a golfer, or a girls' coach?"

Quinn's eyes held hers with a look of such challenging honesty, she knew she couldn't hold back. She looked nervously away, her eyes flicking from the picnic basket to the suntan lotion to the cassette player. She studied the buttons, hoping for a sign, an omen. PLAY, suggested one button, but she couldn't brush off his question with a flippant answer, not when he talked to her about heart-stunning grace. REVERSE, read the next button, but it was too late to go back. EDIT? He had been honest with her, she couldn't be less than honest with him. FAST FORWARD. She plunged in.

"When I was real little I hated baseball," she confessed for the first time in her life. She waited for a protest, or a patronizing chuckle, but Quinn said nothing. He watched closely, his eyes darkly serious.

"I was terrified of the ball. I know it sounds ridiculous, but Ace would toss a ball to me and I'd put both hands in front of my face and sort of mew at him with both eyes closed. I felt like an absolute worm. Here I had this fantastic father who could make a baseball do just about anything except walk on water, and I was too afraid of it to try to catch it. I knew that if I didn't put my hands up it would hit me right between the eyes. So one day, I finally got my nerve up, and I let it."

"What do you mean?" said Quinn.

"I decided nothing that baseball could do to me could be worse than the humiliation I felt, so the next time Ace tossed the ball at me I put my hands behind my back and let it hit me. For a week after that I had an egg in the middle of my forehead, but I wasn't afraid anymore."

Quinn grinned at her and wrinkled his nose in a way that was positively endearing. "I love a kid with guts." He reached across the space between them to stroke the back of her hand with his thumb. "And then?" he prompted.

"I must have been nine when I decided I was going to play for the Yankees. Keep it in the family. I was Ace's only heir, so it was up to me. I practiced like a maniac, but by the time I was ten I knew they'd never let me. That's why Ace sneaked me into the dugout— as a consolation. But I was the world's most inconsolable ten-year-old. It was so crushingly unfair that there was something half of humanity could do, but I couldn't, and just because I was a girl. And that's when it hit me—like that ball between the eyes. I might not be allowed even to try out for the Yankees, but there was nothing to stop me from writing about them. Don't ever tell me there's something I can't do, Quinn. Because sure as anything, I'll go right out and do it."

"I'll remember that," said Quinn. He rolled over on his back and held his open book up against the sun.

She sat up to rub more suntan lotion into her legs. She couldn't keep her eyes off him. It was the whales that did it. Quinn wore a blue French bikini with spouting red whales printed all over it. She knew it was French because she'd read the label when she divided their clean laundry. She didn't have to imagine what it barely covered. She had only to follow the whales.

SHE HAD NEVER PRIDED HERSELF on possessing a particularly acute feminine intuition, but one night after work, as she climbed the stairs to her apartment, she was overcome by the conviction that Quinn was finally gone. She couldn't explain how she knew, she just knew. He had packed up his perfectly creased jeans, and his shaving kit, his portable shortwave radio and his copy of the BBC's "London Calling" and all his cameras and left for his own apartment. She was alone at last. Quinn was out of her life. She knew it deep in her marrow, and it made her knees feel like Play-Doh so she sat on the stairs until they turned back into bones. *It's what I wanted, isn't it?* she asked herself. *I don't fit into his life and he doesn't fit into mine. We're a couple of loners. Aren't we?* You bet!

She raced up the last flight of stairs, opened both locks in record time and threw open the door, calling, "Quinn? Quinn? Are you here?"

The brightness in the room made her blink. All the furniture huddled in the center of the floor beneath a plastic dropcloth. The ceiling was white, the woodwork was white, the walls a soft delicate yellow, like jonquils on a misty morning. Everything sparkled with light.

"Hi!" said Quinn, stepping out of the bathroom. He wore nothing but a towel tucked around his hips. His hair and face and forearms were speckled with paint. "I took the day off. What do you think?"

She didn't know whether to laugh or cry, and her throat had gone impossibly tight. "Oh, Quinn," she finally managed, "it's beautiful, it's . . . well, it's just beautiful."

"Glad you like it, ma'am. We aim to please."

"You didn't have to do this. I don't know what to say."

"I wanted to do something to say thank you for putting up with me. You've been really great about this. But I'll be out of your hair by tomorrow night, with any luck."

"You will?" Her heart fell into her shoes.

"I have this really hot tip for a sub-rosa sublet down on Sixty-second and an appointment to check it out tomorrow. The price is right, and it's just till the end of the year. It should be perfect."

"That's great," she said, wishing for his sake she sounded more enthusiastic, and at the same time wondering why she wasn't. She did want him out, didn't she?

Quinn hitched up his towel. "Give me a couple of minutes to clean up, and I'll take you to—"

"Hamburger Heaven?" she said.

"How did you guess?"

As soon as she heard the shower running she picked up the phone and called Mo.

"He's leaving," she said. "It sounds like this time he has a really solid lead on a place."

"I'll bet you're relieved," said Mo.

"Mo, he painted the living room today. It's beautiful."

"That's nice. What else did he do?"

"What else should he do?"

"Make love to you, of course. What has he been waiting for? That's what I want to know."

"We have an understanding about that. I don't have room for that in my life just now, and neither does he."

"If that's true why do you sound so miserable now that he's about to make his long-anticipated exit?"

"Do I sound miserable?"

"Like you've lost your best friend. Rainey, why don't you stop fighting and let Mother Nature take her own sweet and sexy course?"

"He crowds me, Mo. I think about him all the time, and it's driving me crazy. Mo, I need my space."

"What good is space when you're the only one in it?"

3

"ARCHER. RAI-NEY ARR-CHUR!" Wolfe's bellow met her as she got off the elevator the next morning.

She raced to his desk.

"Want a prune Danish?" said Wolfe. "I've got an extra prune Danish here somewhere." He dragged open a bottom desk drawer and tossed her a grease-stained bag.

"Why, thanks," she said, startled by his unexpected generosity.

"Take it and sit down. I'm giving you a special assignment."

"Hmm?" She poked the Danish. It was as hard as a dog biscuit. Wolfe's wife bred schnauzers. Maybe it *was* a dog biscuit. She asked herself whether it was really a dog biscuit, or if New York was finally making her as crazy and suspicious as everyone else. Was this what living with Quinn had done to her?

Wolfe said, "I want you to do a color story on a ballet dancer."

"Me? *Me*?" She laughed nervously. "Don't kid around, Wolfe, it's been a tough week, and Friday's barely begun." She was a sportswriter, not a culture-vulture reporter.

"Our publisher's beautiful and talented wife, Lillian, thinks you'd be—" He pursed his lips into a winsome, if bristly Marilyn Monroe pout. "*Wooo-wondur-ful!* She's a big patron of American Ballet Studio, our Lillian. Mooches around on their board, organizes fund drives. You know the sort of thing. She's just plain crazy for ballet. And after three years of pestering she's finally browbeaten some Russian commissar of culture into letting their newest hotshot dancer come to New York to dance with her company for a fund-raiser. Cultural exchange, goodwill ambassador, etcetera, etcetera."

"But why does the beautiful and talented Lillian want me?" Every reporter on the staff lived in terror of the day when the publisher's wife might notice him and suggest some harebrained story to that hapless reporter's editor. Rainey had assumed sports blessedly safe from her depredations. "I can't believe she combs the sports pages for my byline."

"No, but she did read your series on the figure skating championships in Innsbruck. Then someone gave her a book called, *Dance Is a Contact Sport*, and that started her off. She likes, and I'm quoting here, the way you 'write about bodies in space,' or something."

"Oh, Wolfe," Rainey groaned. "I thought you were finally going to give me a baseball story."

He shook his head and sighed heavily. "Not yet. Maybe later in the season. Meanwhile, this dancer is all set up for you. Your first interview is scheduled to follow a cattle-call press conference this afternoon. Then you and your photog are cleared to observe tomorrow's rehearsal. The dance critic will cover the gala Tuesday night, and that wraps it up. Okay? One o'clock this afternoon at American Ballet Studio. And take Fletcher."

"I'd rather take Quinn."

"Yeah? Well, it figures. I heard you two were living together."

"It's nothing like that, Wolfe. I'm just putting him up on my sofa until he can find a place of his own."

"Sure," said Wolfe with infuriating smugness. "So take Quinn, he'll bring in some good stuff."

"What's her name, the dancer?"

"It's not a her, it's a him." He glanced at a blue assignment slip before handing it to her. "Kuprin. Aleksey Maximovitch Kuprin, *premier danseur*, Leningrad Kirov Ballet."

"Is that better than the other one, the Bolshoi?"

"You're asking the wrong guy."

"Wolfe, I have to tell you, I don't feel altogether comfortable with this. I probably haven't been to the ballet more than six times in my entire life, and you know I want to start digging out background material for a series on drug testing in the minor leagues, and—"

Wolfe closed his eyes, effectively cutting off all further communication. "Go!" he intoned, his rumbling bass heavy with phony menace. "Take your sneakers off my desk and get out of here."

She went to call Quinn in the photography department.

"You almost missed me," he said. "I'm on my way to look at the sublet. Why don't you come along?"

"I'll meet you downstairs in the lobby in three minutes," she said. "Load up on film, we've got an assignment this afternoon."

As the elevator doors closed she heard Wolfe calling, "*Arr-churr!* You forgot your prune Danish."

THE APARTMENT BUILDING was a white marble and bronze beehive, fifty-stories high, immaculate and gleaming.

Rainey said, "It looks like an awfully cold building to me. I mean, it doesn't have any history. Not like a brownstone. Brownstones are full of history. Living here must be like living in a file drawer. I'll bet all the rooms are painted manila."

No battered mailboxes here. A Persian carpet the size of Montana bloomed intricately beneath crystal chandeliers. A gracious concierge directed them to the express elevator to the forty-seventh floor. Vivaldi chirped softly in the whirring elevator.

Rainey said, "You'd never get me to live this high up. If there was a fire, you'd never make it out."

Quinn grinned at her as the bronze doors opened and they stepped out into the hall. "C'mon, Champ. You haven't even seen the place yet. I think it's great. I had a place just like this in Paris a couple of years ago."

"You went to Paris and you lived in a place like this? God, that's really depressing. I thought photographers had romance in their souls." She followed Quinn down the hall, saying, "How could you possibly afford a place like this? You'll never get your alimony paid off if you take this place."

Quinn pressed the bell at 47-O. "The building doesn't allow sublets. I'm supposed to be the house-sitter. It's incredibly cheap. All hush-hush and under the table."

"Come in, come in, come in!" cawed a slight, bird-like woman. She hopped back from the door. "I'm Josie Dentici. I hope you're a plant person, Mr. Quinn. This," said Miss Dentici, a single gesture encompassing all before them, "this is my little garden."

Green and growing things were everywhere: plants, shrubs, trees, spread urgent foliage in every direction. Palms reared up to snatch at creeping ivies inching across the ceiling. Succulents bulged, miniature oranges gleamed beneath their Gro-Lites. The air was moist and heavy with the scent of waxy gardenia bushes, verbena and mulch. Sap plopped in the stillness. A bank of ficus sighed into a Boston fern.

Rainey tugged at Quinn's sleeve. "It looks like Plants-R-Us," she whispered.

Skirting the two director's chairs in the center of the room, Miss Dentici said, "Everything on this wall is watered on Mondays. These over here on Wednesdays. Those on Saturdays. All leaves are to be misted each morning. On the third Friday of each month you

will mix up five gallons of Green-n-Gro. It's their little extra tonic. They love it so." She swooped to pluck
a yellowing leaf from a wax begonia. "On Sundays
you wipe the leaves with surgical cotton moistened
with Plant Bath, examining the undersides for aphids
and scale. You must take extraordinary care not to
overwater, of course. Root rot is so insidious."

"Where do you . . . that is, where's the bedroom?"
said Rainey.

Quinn's mouth opened, but nothing came out.

"Bedroom?" Miss Dentici looked quite dumbfounded by the question.

Rainey was sure she slept hanging upside down
from a banana palm.

"There is no bedroom. I keep a futon, a Japanese
mattress, in the hall closet. When you push these
chairs back under the philodendron and pull the
bamboo trees over toward the giant jades, there's
plenty of room for a futon. Will you take it, Mr.
Quinn?"

Rainey tugged at Quinn's sleeve. "You can't sleep on
a crouton."

"I can't?"

"You'll wake up in the morning covered with leaf
mold. You'll mildew." She turned to Miss Dentici. "I'm
sorry, but Mr. Quinn understood you had a bedroom. He really needs a bedroom."

Miss Dentici glanced from Quinn to Rainey and
back to Quinn. "Yes," she said with asperity. "I expect
you do. However . . ." Her mouth compressed to a

lipless slit. "I don't sublet to lecherous men and their loose women. It's out of the question, Mr. Quinn. And as for you, miss, I wouldn't entrust you with a pot of alfalfa."

"Now just a damned minute—" Rainey began, her cheeks burning, but Quinn hustled her out, still sputtering, and into a cab.

"C'mon," he urged. "You'll be late for your dancer." Once in the cab he said, "I don't understand you. I don't understand you at all. I bust my buns trying to find an apartment, and then you queer the deal. I thought you wanted me out of your hair."

"I do, but—"

"Well, I would have taken the place. Crouton, or no crouton."

"And live in that jungle?"

He gave her a long, sleepy look. "It reminded me of Borneo, and I liked Borneo."

"Quinn, did you see the marks on her neck? I'll bet she was bitten by a fruit bat."

"HOW WOULD YOU LIKE to sink your teeth into that?" murmured Quinn.

"Into what?" Rainey clicked a blank cassette into her tape recorder.

"Not what, Champ, *who*. Look over there. Aleksey Kuprin just walked in. The Leaping Lion of Leningrad. Tell me the truth, is that your sort of guy?"

"Shut up, Quinn," she said.

Down at the front of the recital hall, a buzzing swarm of ballet company officials hovered around a man clad all in black—black T-shirt, black jeans, black shoes. A black dance bag hung from his bulging shoulder. Beside him loomed a Slavic version of a sumo wrestler who had to be his bodyguard. The chairman of the ballet's board made a brief introduction, reading from notes, and retreated from the glare of the lights.

Aleksey Kuprin stepped forward, slung his dance bag to the floor, hooked his thumbs in his jeans and stood with chin high and feet splayed, emanating raw elemental power and raw elemental sex. A hush fell over the roomful of reporters and photographers: press down front, network TV in the back, local minicams at the sides, all were silent. He cocked his head, taking them all in with one long, smoldering glance—it was a superbly haughty look, proud, brave, a trifle insolent, yet vulnerable, for all its bravado—like a matador who turns his back on the bull to acknowledge the ovation of ten thousand cheering throats.

Spontaneously, everyone applauded.

"Olé!" Rainey said to Quinn who wrinkled his nose. "That," she murmured to Quinn, "is style."

Quinn snorted. "That's not style. That's theater."

Kuprin bowed, smiled, and the press conference began. Rainey watched and waited. She'd have him to herself when this was over. She turned on her tape recorder, listened with half an ear and studied him with cool interest. She had never seen a dancer out of costume before. He wasn't built like any one athlete she could think of, but rather combined several in unexpected ways. He had the strongly corded neck and shoulders of a pole vaulter, the cleanly muscled arms and chest of a gymnast, a swimmer's narrow waist and hips, the powerful driving thighs of a speedskater, and the tough, square hands of a quarterback. A month ago she would have thought him gorgeous, but today, compared to the sight of Quinn with a towel slung around his hips and paint in his hair, Kuprin didn't even make the cut for her list of Ten Greatest Looking Guys.

The questions continued. "How do you like New York, Mr. Kuprin?"

"I do not know. I am arrived only since last night."

"Why haven't you performed in the West before? This can't be the first time you've been invited?"

A rookie's shy grin and a shrug from Kuprin. "I dance where my government wants me to dance." His eyes swept the room restlessly until they came to rest on Rainey, and to her they returned after each question.

"Why is he staring at you?" whispered Quinn.

"Is he?" Kuprin smiled at her with the supreme confidence of an ace-relief pitcher. Her palms suddenly felt sticky. *Why me?* she wondered.

The questions went on and on.

"Quinn," said Rainey. "Is it a trick of the lights, or does Kuprin make Baryshnikov look positively puny?"

Quinn smirked. "Checking him out? Imagining your little Aleksey keeping the chill off your back through a lo-o-ong Russian night? The two of you wrapped in black sable making love on the floor in front of the samovar—"

"What do you mean *little* Aleksey?"

"He's very short," hissed Quinn.

"Oh, go check your strobe," said Rainey. How could Quinn be so irritating when she'd just saved him from life in a bat-infested jungle?

When the news conference broke up, Quinn ran interference for Rainey, and they worked their way down to the front of the hall against the oncoming tide of exiting media. Among all those faces she didn't see a single one she knew. They were all arts writers or dance mavins.

"Good afternoon, Mr. Kuprin," she said, extending her hand. Quinn was right. The top of Kuprin's head came up to her chin. "My name is Rainey Archer. I'm ah . . . I'm ah . . ." The man had a grip like a boa constrictor. She needed that hand to type. She squeezed back. His eyes opened wide. They were a deep smoky topaz, like a tiger's eyes. A crafty Siberian tiger's eyes.

Kuprin cleared his throat, his feet came together, and before her astonished eyes he seemed to grow a foot taller as his body arched over her hand. From his toes to his crown, he became a gracious curve of spring-steel. It was not Kuprin, but the Swan Prince who held her hand as though it were a swan feather, and brushed it with his lips murmuring, "*Enchanté*, Mademoiselle."

"I'm from the *New York Journal*," she finally managed. She introduced Quinn and turned to the bull-necked man beside Kuprin. Close up, he looked like a world-class weight lifter who ate rosin bags for lunch. She put out her hand to him. His eyes were the depthless gray of old aluminum, and they did not blink.

"And you are?" she prompted.

"Boris Sergeyevitch Tolinkov. Buddyguard." He pumped her hand, adding, "Waluable fellow, our Aleksey Maximovitch, we want nothing should befall him."

Kuprin laughed, and his diaphragm muscles rippled and pulsed. The red I Love New York slogan on his black T-shirt bobbled up and down.

"You are liking shirt?" He had caught her looking. He grinned and thumped his chest proudly. "I am making official welcoming delegation halt at airport store. I am choosing shirt. Boris is buying cushion for Irina, his wife."

She glanced at Boris. He might have been smiling. On the other hand, the rosin bags might have been giving him gas. Quinn's busy shutter whirred. Only the ballet's publicity staff hovered in a semicircle just out of range, everyone else had left.

"Mr. Kuprin," Rainey began, "would you like to talk here?" She gestured toward the first row of newly vacated seats. "Or, would you like to—" His eyes captured hers again; they were dark with silent pleading.

He collapsed into a seat, clutching his belly with one hand and his head with the other.

"What's wrong?" she said urgently. "Can you tell me what's wrong?"

Kuprin's retinue closed around them like a cloak. Quinn stood on a chair, his motor-driven shutter chugging away.

Kuprin groaned. *"Boizhemoi!* I am suffering jets lag. Great sinking here." He tapped his hard belly. She half expected it to resonate like a kettle drum.

J. J. Peters, the ballet company's publicity chief, a chubby man with a polished, pink and shining head, spoke to no one in particular. "I said an interview after the press conference was a *bad thing*. But Kuprin insisted." He turned to Rainey. "It's too much. Too much. He only came in last night. He took class this morning with everyone else, and he's been rehearsing ever since. It's too much. But he insisted. I said it was a *bad thing*." Rainey patted his arm. He looked close to tears.

"Ach!" spat Boris. "Aleksey Maximovitch is strong like bull." But his eyes were dark with concern.

Aleksey Maximovitch looked up at her with jet-weary eyes. He was visibly wilting, his limbs loose, his muscles slack, his hands inert. He was a puppet whose strings had been cut.

Rainey tried to remember the name of the ballet she had seen in which the puppets collapsed. Was it *Petroushka*? *Coppélia*? She looked at him closely. If it didn't seem so small-minded, she would swear he was over overacting.

Kuprin reached out to touch her hand. "Is okay we talk later, please? Tonight, maybe?"

"Now that would be a *good thing*," said J. J. Peters. "A *very good thing*." To Rainey he said, "Could you meet Mr. Kuprin here at nine o'clock?"

"Perhaps tomorrow?" she suggested. "Before or after the rehearsal. We're supposed to cover a rehearsal tomorrow."

"No, emphatically not." Peters shook his head and ticked off Kuprin's schedule on his fingers. "Tomorrow he takes class, followed by a *closed* rehearsal, followed by two days' rest in Alexandria, Virginia, with the Soviet ambassador and his family, then rehearsal and performance on Tuesday, then whoosh! Away."

"Whoosh, away?" Rainey said.

Kuprin laughed. "I dance *Giselle* in Leningrad on Thursday. Albrecht," he added with a clarifying smile.

She glanced at Quinn. Quinn, shrugged and crouching, backed away, shooting as he went.

"Tonight at nine, then," she said.

Kuprin rose like a flame. "Good. Thank you." He turned to Boris. "I am better now. We go." At the door, he turned on his heel and strode back to her, rummaging in his dance bag as he came. "I am forgetting . . . forgive me. Lillian is begging me give you memento. She says you are too shy to be asking yourself." His eyes, no longer hooded and weary, blazed at her, and before she could think of something to say he jammed a pair of broken-down practice shoes into her hands. "Nine o'clock. Do not forget." He smiled over his shoulder as he headed for the knot of arguing retainers in the hall.

Is this Friday the thirteenth? she asked herself sourly. First, Wolfe strong-armed her into taking an assignment she didn't want, then Quinn starts needling her because she messed up his apartment deal—when in fact he should be grateful, and now this dancer with the cocker spaniel eyes gives her his beat-up old shoes—sweaty, tired old rags of black leather.

"Tell me the truth," she said to Quinn. They were in a cab going back downtown to the *Journal.* "Do I look like a weirdo? Why in the world would he dump his old shoes on me?"

"It's an honor. Don't you know anything? Giving shoes is an old ballet custom."

"How do you know that?" she asked suspiciously.

"I read it in the *New Yorker.* Dedicated admirers beg and grovel for dancers' discarded shoes."

"You read the *New Yorker*?"

"I was waiting for my dentist. Let me see."

"They're hardly shoes at all, look." She dug them out of her bag, handed one to Quinn and examined the other. "No padding, no support, zip. They're nothing. They're like kid gloves for the feet, or leather socks."

Quinn crushed the other shoe into a ball. "If you think of those leaps they do and all the jumps and spins . . ." He whistled under his breath. "You know, if a basketball player came down from a slam-dunk and hit the floor in these shoes he'd shatter everything from dah foot bones to dah neck bones. You have to hand it to them. Dancers are tough."

"They must be," Rainey agreed. She poked under the sweat-stained insole and the insole fell into her lap. "Oh, my God!" she all but screamed. "Look, Quinn, look!"

Printed in careful capitals in the bottom of the shoe she read: "HELP ME I WANT TO DEFECT PLEASE."

4

"HOW LONG WILL IT TAKE YOU to write this up?" said Quinn. His eyes flashed with excitement. Impatiently he punched the button for their floor. They had the elevator to themselves. "I can have my prints ready in the blink of an eye. If you can get your story through the copy desk by late deadline, we can still make the second street edition. Give me that shoe. I have to have a shot of the message in the shoe. I can throw it on a copy stand and slap a sheet of glass over it. Nothing to it. Give me the shoe . . ."

"No," said Rainey thoughtfully.

"DANCER BEGS AID . . ." He sketched the headline in the air.

"I don't think so."

"KING OF KIROV DESPERATE FOR FREEDOM . . . What do you mean No?" Quinn demanded.

The elevator doors parted revealing two reporters and a copy boy stepping forward. Rainey jabbed the Close button, and the trio disappeared in midstride.

"You've got it wrong, Quinn." She jambed her thumb on the Lobby button. "The head on my story—"

"Your story? What do you mean, your story? Our story!"

"The headline is going to be DANCER DEFECTS."

"You're crazier than I thought. Give me that shoe."

The lobby appeared. Quinn lunged for the Close button. Rainey swiveled her hips, executed a lightning T'ai Chi sidestep and slipped out of the elevator while his finger was still a foot from the button.

"I need time to think this through," she called over her shoulder to an astonished Quinn. "If you want to talk about it, I'll be at Doyle's." She strode out onto Forty-third Street and headed west.

"HOW DO YOU DEFECT?" said Rainey, blowing gently on her coffee. "Do you go to the nearest precinct house, or what?"

"Not the cops," offered Quinn. "Remember Medved, the sailor who tried to jump ship in New Orleans? The cops sent him back. Twice."

"I thought that was the Coast Guard," said Rainey.

"Yeah? I thought it was the local cops." Quinn crunched a pretzel. "Immigration, Champ, I'm sure you have to go to Immigration."

"They must be in the book," said Rainey. "I'll call and ask."

"But why?" Quinn's dark eyes flickered with suspicion. "You still haven't told me why." He drank off the last of the beer in his glass and set it on the bar for Doyle to refill. "We've got a perfectly good, clean story here. An exclusive! Why not go with it? How can you justify withholding it? Why risk losing a good story in order to get mixed up in what is bound to be a very iffy sort of thing?" He held his hand flat, palm down, at chest level and waggled it. "Very iffy."

"It's the right thing to do, Quinn. . . ."

"And suddenly you're Joan of Arc?" He waved a warning finger in front of her nose. "Remember what happened to Joan of Arc."

"Aleksey Kuprin is a sensitive artist living under an oppressive government—"

"C'mon, Champ. You're a hard-bitten reporter, not a jelly-hearted social worker. You're as tough as an alligator's knees, so don't give me all that bull about oppressed artists."

"How can you be so dense, Quinn? Don't you see that a ballet dancer wanting to defect isn't news? Who wouldn't want to defect if they saw a glimmer of a chance to get out of Soviet Russia? On the other hand, the Kirov's hot prodigy actually defecting—with the help of a *New York Journal* sportswriter—"

Quinn peered at her sharply and cleared his throat. "And maybe a *New York Journal* photographer," she amended. "Now that would be a real story. Don't you see? It's the perfect exclusive every reporter sees in her dreams."

Quinn rubbed his chin thoughtfully. He chewed a pretzel. He scowled meditatively at the polished bar. He crunched another pretzel, washed it down, then flashed her a ten-thousand-megawatt grin. "You know something? You're right, Champ. It kills me to say it, but you're right."

"Oh, say it again, Quinn. I love to hear you say it."

Quinn ignored her. "This could be one helluva story. The National desk will eat it up."

"Not National desk," Rainey insisted. "And it won't go to the Metro desk either. It's going to go to the Sports desk. Lillian, Mrs. Publisher, wanted Kuprin covered as an athlete, didn't she?"

Quinn nodded.

"So this story, *our* story goes to Wolfe. It's going to be the biggest story he's had since he broke the point-shaving scandal."

"Aren't you forgetting something?"

"What?" she said.

"Your would-be defector is rehearsing tomorrow—a rehearsal from which the press is barred, you may remember. Then he's slated to loll away a couple of days with his ambassador down in Washington, then another day of rehearsal, the performance and, as that anxious rabbit Peters put it, they stuff him into an Aeroflot jet and 'whoosh away.' You get one chance at him—you interview him tonight at nine, and that's that. After the gala they'll see to it he disappears up the chimney faster than a squirrel with a singed tail. How do you think you can help him? Mobilize a bunch of your chums from St. Scholastica's and snatch him from the ambassador's swimming pool? It can't be done."

"Who says?" she demanded.

"I say. Sure, it's got potential as a story, but a potential story is not a story, it's a pipe dream." He spoke gently, reasonably, but she was in no mood to be reasoned with. "Give it up, Champ," he urged softly.

"My chums, as you put it, are all either out of the country or just plain out of town, as it happens, except for Mo, of course. So I'm going to have to manage this myself. However, if you want to help me with this, *and* get some great shots, *and* share the credit, that's fine with me. But if you want out, that's okay with me too, because I'm going to find a way to get that guy away from his keeper—from that Boris creep." She took a deep breath and said, "Don't you see? Kuprin is my ticket out of swimming meets, out of fifty-meter freestyle and backstrokes and butterflies and that awful water polo. Oh, how I hate the stink of chlorine. I want to spend the rest of my working life in the sun—smelling the grass and the hotdogs and the peanuts. Aleksey Kuprin is going to get me into the press box at Yankee Stadium. This story is going to make me look so good to Wolfe, and Wolfe look so good to the publisher, that he won't be able to say no."

"You'd go out on a limb to help this guy just to get a chance to write about the Yankees?"

"There's almost nothing I wouldn't do," she said through clenched teeth, "to write about the Yankees."

He whistled under his breath. "I don't suppose there's anything a mere rational man could say to stop you."

"You're right, Quinn, there's not a thing."

Quinn studied her thoughtfully for a time, shaking his head slowly but eloquently from side to side. At last he said, "I must be as crazy as you are, but I'm with you."

"You are? Really?" She could hardly believe it. She very nearly threw her arms around him and kissed him. Quinn actually opting to work with her could only mean he believed they could pull it off. She only wished *she* really believed they could do it. "Thanks," she said, gratefully. "Thanks a lot." She grinned back at him.

"Now when do we let Wolfe in on this?"

"We don't," she said.

"But don't you tell your editor everything? Isn't that press protocol or something?"

"Give me a break, Quinn. If Wolfe knew about this he'd pull me off the story and give it someone like Billings. No way! This is *mine*," she added fiercely.

"You've really got guts," he said, his black eyes somehow trapping hers.

Why was he looking at her like that? It was the way he'd looked at her on the plane, just before he'd kissed her. And a couple of times in the park, and once after they'd watched *Casablanca* on the *Late Show*. It wasn't how crusty, cynical photographers looked at sportswriters who were as tough as alligators' knees. She looked away first.

"Well, now," she began, oddly nervous. Why should Quinn suddenly make her feel so . . . so . . .

skittish? She finished her coffee before looking at him again. "The first thing we have to do is find out how he defects. Maybe we can fix it up for after the interview. Order me another cup of coffee, and I'll call Immigration." She slid off the bar stool and headed for the phone at the back.

"Immigration and Naturalization Service," said a precise, reedy tenor.

Rainey cleared her throat and said, "I would like some information, please, about the proper procedure for a um..." She searched for a word that wouldn't give everything away, she daren't say Russian. "For a foreign national who is in this country temporarily, but would like to stay." She congratulated herself on how diplomatically she put it.

"For private reasons or political ones?"

"Political and private, I guess," said Rainey.

"Is the country of origin Eastern or Western?"

"Eastern."

"I see." Ominous pause. "And would this be a possible defection or a request for asylum?"

She could feel her throat tightening with frustration. "What difference does it make? It's someone who wants to stay in America."

"But it makes a great deal of difference. Defections go to Special Services, Window Seven, asylums to Window Four."

"Window Seven? You handle defections at a window?"

"There are forms to fill out, questions to be answered. It's not so simple as everyone seems to imagine. We have to determine whether he or she meets the statutory standards under which the government grants political asylum. There are questions of presumption of persecution under a totalitarian government. I take it this person is from a totalitarian country?"

"Yes."

"Then, of course, there's the refugee status to be considered . . . Special Services is open from nine till five, Monday through Friday."

Her heart sank. This was Friday and nearly five. "But I thought someone wanting to defect just called you people up and you met that person someplace and took him into protective custody, or whatever, and that was that. Don't you do that?"

"Only in the movies. If it's cloak-and-dagger capers you're looking for, you're welcome to try the State Department in Washington. But if we're closing in four minutes, they're closing in four minutes."

"Closing? How can you close? What about your country's pledge to welcome the downtrodden and oppressed? Don't you care about your country's pledge? What happened to 'give me your tempest-tossed?' And 'I lift my lamp beside the golden door'?"

"Young lady," he began, his voice thin and prickly, "you are not talking to Emma Goldman. You are talking to the Civil Service. We will be happy to process your tempest-tossed at nine o'clock on Monday morning."

"That's it? That's all you have to say?"

"Have a nice day."

Disconsolate, Rainey walked slowly back to the bar. "No game," she said to Quinn. "We've been rained out."

"As bad as that? What did they say?"

She told him. Quinn studied the thinning head on his beer. Rainey stared glumly at her father's picture on the wall behind the bar. His Yankee uniform hung on his lanky frame. The creased bill of his cap cast a crescent of shadow over his eyes. His big, boyish grin was stretched over a lopsided bulge, because he never pitched without wadding his cheek full of gum. He had always smelled of cinnamon. His gloved right hand rested on his hip, and with his pitching arm he hugged Bobby Doyle, his catcher during those glory years when they had played for the Yankees.

"I have to wonder...." Quinn began. He didn't speak to her directly, but fixed his attention on the bottles behind the bar.

Quinn, she decided, had what their drama critic would call a strong profile. She, on the other hand, saw it as more than strong—it was rugged, with thick black brows, a straight nose above a full, sensitive mouth, and a stubborn, jutting chin. A very stubborn chin. And at his temple she could just detect the slow, steady beat of his pulse. *Pum . . . pum . . . pum.*

"I wonder," he began again, "if you're so anxious to help Kuprin just for the story and the chance to get your own typewriter at Yankee Stadium...."

Rainey was dumbfounded. "What other reason could there be?"

"He's not such a bad-looking guy," Quinn suggested.

"There are those who would say he's not unattractive," she conceded.

"I watched him, all smarmy, kissing your hand—"

"He's not smarmy. Hand-kissing is an elegant, old-world courtesy. I'm surprised you haven't read about it in the *New Yorker*."

Quinn ignored her jibe. "He looks like a cut-rate clone of Baryshnikov. He could probably pass for Baryshnikov—in the dark with the light behind him. There are busloads of women out there who'd walk barefoot over burning *Playbill*'s to get their mitts on a guy like Kuprin. The locker room scuttlebutt is that some of these dancers have more notches on their jocks than pop stars." His eyes were still fixed on the bottles, but the blue fluttering vein in his temple was going, *Pa-pum, pa-pum, pa-pum, pa-pum, pa-pum*.

"Quinn," she said, smiling to herself. "Some men send out signals so primitive, so basic no woman can resist them. They speak to primal urges deep within us. They tug at our—"

"Stop!" He spun around on his bar stool, his eyes blazing furiously. "I don't care what he's tugging at. But I'll tell you one thing, Champ. He's a phony."

"Not," she said airily, "where elemental passions are concerned."

"Elemental passions?" Quinn chuckled, "You know, Champ, I think your greatest asset as a reporter is that you can lie like the very devil and still look as guileless as Goldilocks."

She grinned sheepishly. Of course she was lying. Compared to Quinn, Kuprin was about as exciting as a haddock. But how did Quinn know she was lying? Was he watching a pulse in *her* temple?

For a long time they sat silently side by side. Then Rainey said, "What if I cozy up to Peters, that public relations guy tonight. I'm all sweetness and light, and I suggest it would be sensational to do my interview while giving Kuprin a tour of the city."

"Not bad," said Quinn. "KIROV STAR VISITS NEW YORK BY NIGHT—with pix by me—"

"And questions by me—"

"And reactions and comments by Kuprin," he concluded.

"We could do it, Quinn. We could. All we have to do is ditch Boris someplace and keep Kuprin out of sight until we can present him at Window Seven at nine o'clock on Monday morning."

"Stash him someplace and stay with him until Monday," said Quinn thoughtfully.

"Mo's place?" she said.

"Your advertising friend? But where will she be?"

"She always goes to Connecticut for the weekend."

"You're forgetting something," said Quinn.

"What?"

"Boris."

"You're right," she said gloomily. "How do we get him to look the other way long enough for us to spirit Kuprin out from under his hairy nose?"

Quinn shook his head and munched a pretzel thoughtfully.

"Could you drink him under the table?" she offered brightly.

"Are you kidding? The man's only one size smaller than a John Deere tractor."

"I just wondered.... Pass the pretzels."

"Doyle!" chortled Quinn. "Doyle could put Boris away for us. Doyle could slip Boris a Mickey."

"He wouldn't do that."

"Not for me, he wouldn't. But he'd do it for you. Ask him," said Quinn. "Hey, Doyle," he called down the bar. "Rainey wants to ask you a favor."

"Whatever you want, it's yours, honey," said Doyle, leaning his freckled arms on the bar. His blue eyes were fond and smiling. He was a big-boned man, beefy with retirement, as deliberate in his movements as her father had been whippet-fast.

"Uncle Bobby," she said, "if Quinn and I were to walk in here tonight with a couple of guys and we wanted to get one of them out of the way for a while— say a couple of hours—could you slip him a Mickey?"

Doyle thought it over for ten, eleven seconds. "For you? Sure. Do you want I should leave him in the back with the beer crates to sleep it off, or should maybe a couple of the guys dump him someplace quiet like?"

Quinn said, "The park would be nice."

"That would be perfect," Rainey agreed. "There's one other little thing. Uncle Bobby, can I borrow your car until Monday morning?"

His face crumpled. "First it's a Mickey, now it's my car. Rainey, honey, you don't know what you're asking."

"C'mon, Doyle," wheedled Quinn. "Champ here really needs it."

Doyle reached across the bar to lay a huge, callused hand on her hair. "Sure, kid. Go ahead." He was grinning now. "But don't press your luck, hey?"

Rainey raced to the phone to call Mo.

"YOU ARE LIKING SHOES?" Kuprin's eyes were wide with anxious questions.

"Very much," she said, hoping her eyes conveyed more than she dared put into words. "They were a . . . revelation."

Kuprin nodded and dropped into a chair.

Rainey and Quinn had walked into the ballet's publicity office on the dot of nine to find Kuprin pacing nervously, Boris lurking in a corner and J. J. Peters hovering attentively, if palely, over Kuprin. Peters looked exhausted, all pinkness gone, his face ashen.

"Mr. Kuprin, Mr. Peters," she began, and launched into an enthusiastic, if somewhat expurgated, description of their plan to take Kuprin out for a photogenic night on the town. She paused to sketch tomorrow's headline in the air between them. "KIROV STAR VISITS NEW YORK BY NIGHT. It'll make a terrific story," she concluded breathlessly.

"*Da! Da! Da!*" Kuprin exploded, bouncing out of his chair.

Peters listened raptly, the haggard look draining from his face as she spoke. "You mean you'll take them off my hands, I mean out on the town? Both of them? Mr. Kuprin and Boris? And you won't need me?" He was almost pleading.

"We can handle everything," Quinn assured him.

"No problem," she added.

"What a splendid idea," said Peters, a tinge of pink returning to his cheeks. "I don't mind telling you, I've been running myself ragged over this gala, and there's still so much to do. I can't tell you how grateful I'd be if you can manage this without me. That would be such a *good thing*."

"I'm sure," said Rainey emphatically, "that it will be a sensational interview." She smiled like Goldilocks.

Quinn clapped Peters on the shoulder and said, "In years to come, you'll look back on this interview as one of the most memorable you ever promoted."

"Then as far as I'm concerned it's settled," Peters said almost gaily. "Mr. Kuprin and Boris are staying at the Soviet's U.N. Mission. I'm sure I can safely say their car and driver are at your disposal."

"Their car?" said Quinn.

"Their driver?" said Rainey.

"We thought—" Quinn began.

"A cab," finished Rainey. Dealing with Boris was going to be difficult enough, but a car with a Russian driver? How would they get rid of the driver, too?

Quinn touched her arm. A swift, reassuring tap. "That's very kind of you," he said to Peters. "But we really don't need a driver."

Peters passed a hand over his weary eyes. "Enjoy it, my dears. I don't think you have much choice."

"*BOIZHEMOI!* Is beautiful city," marveled Kuprin. "Very beautiful."

"But decadent," corrected Boris with a bulldog scowl.

"Of course is decadent, Boris Sergeyevitch, but is very beautiful."

The big car cruised silently through the city, a sleek black shark nosing its imperious way through schools of taxis. Together, she and Quinn had planned a route that coiled on itself like a snail's shell. At the very center was Doyle's Bar, to which, after a suitable length of time, the four of them would go to quench their thirst—and thirsty work this night of sightseeing and pictures was going to be.

"Pretzel?" she asked Kuprin, as they double-parked in front of the Guggenheim Museum. "Cheezz Krunchies?" she said to Boris. Her shoulder bag rustled with munchies.

She diligently pointed out the usual tourist sights and wrote down Kuprin's impressions, while Quinn photographed him at every stop, and Boris, wolfing Cheezz Krunchies, hovered. Their driver, attached by earphones to a cassette player on the seat beside him, slumped nodding at the steering wheel, his thin, dry lips moving silently. He was learning Italian.

As Quinn captured Kuprin posing dramatically in front of Lincoln Center, Kuprin cast ever more anxious looks at her. She had expected that she or Quinn would have a moment alone with him—a minute, maybe two—enough time to assure him that his trust in them was not misplaced, that they had worked out a plan, a very good plan, for separating him from Boris and assuring his safe defection. But Boris was never out of earshot, so she tried to tell him with her eyes and by giving him the thumbs-up sign when behind Boris's back.

Clucking Russian cautions at him, Boris suffered a grinning Kuprin to perch for Quinn's camera astride a stone lion above the steps of the New York Public Library.

"Is not much," said Boris with a dismissive wave of his meaty hand. "Moscow Library is bigger."

"Hmmnym," said Kuprin, making what she described in her notes as his Thoughtful Russian sound. "Books I am having no time for." He climbed down from the lion and into Boris's waiting arms.

"How do you like to spend your free time?" said Rainey, pencil poised.

"With womens." He leered at Rainey.

"Have some pretzels," she said.

"Love I am making always on my back," he confided.

She looked beseechingly at Quinn who stopped shooting only long enough to raise an eyebrow at her.

Boris broke in. "I tell you secret. All dancers suffer. Bad backs, bad knees. Is from lifting ballerinas. But that you must not print."

"You look light and strong," added Kuprin with a lascivious grin.

"C'mon, Quinn, let's go!" she called to him.

Ten minutes later, Kuprin slouched languidly against the Washington Square Arch. In the two minutes it took Quinn to fire off a dozen shots, a small crowd gathered. Kuprin smiled and cast sidelong, sultry glances at the girls. At least Rainey thought they were girls. In the Village she was never quite sure. Boris moved to cut him out of the throng as neatly as a sheepdog, though not before a young man with magenta hair and diamond stud in his nostril muttered in Kuprin's ear.

"What did the weirdo say to him?" murmured Quinn as they climbed back in the limo.

"He offered him a smorgasbord of mind-altering recreational substances," whispered Rainey.

"And what did our boy say?"

"*Da, da, da, da, da.*"

Quinn rolled his eyes. "Do you think he understood?"

"Da!"

Beneath the marquee for *A Chorus Line* in Schubert Alley, Kuprin executed astonishing pirouettes for Quinn. He looked like an outfielder spinning on wet grass. "Is good dancing, this show," said Kuprin. "Dancer from Danish Ballet tell me this show."

Gazing soulfully at the shipping in the East River he asked, "Is true in river you cannot swim?"

"We have pools," snapped Quinn.

"And Coney Island, too," said Rainey.

With the car purring behind them, they strolled up Fifth Avenue toward Central Park. At Gucci's window Kuprin's mouth fell open and his eyes darkened with raw lust. He touched her arm. "Of what cloth is coat, please?" He pointed to a nubbly, biscuit-colored jacket.

"Raw silk," she said.

Kuprin sighed.

"Is decadent," growled Boris.

"Have a peanut," she said, passing the bag around as they walked. As she cracked her third or fourth peanut she heard Kuprin gasp.

He stared at her, scowling, his eyes puzzled. "To pavement you throw shells?"

"Sure," she said with a shrug, munching another nut.

"Is great offense make dirty Soviet streets."

"Well," said Quinn, "not to worry. We've got these gigantic street sweepers."

"*Da!* We, too." Kuprin laughed and Boris scowled. "We have strong women with brooms."

When the peanuts were gone, Kuprin announced, "I am hungry."

"Hungry?" she said. She was dying of thirst. Why wasn't he dying of thirst? To allay any suspicions Boris might have, the suggestion that they go for a drink had to come from either Kuprin or Boris.

"Dancers always hungry," said Boris, rumbling with laughter. It was the first time she had heard him laugh, and it was not a pleasant experience. He sounded like an express train bursting from a tunnel.

"Big American steak I would like eat," said Kuprin.

"Great idea," said Quinn. "SOVIET'S SIZZLING SIR-LOIN. It should make a good shot."

"But first I would like see typical American barroom. Drink at—saloon? Is *saloon*?"

"*Saloon,*" said Rainey, hoping her emphasis warned him of extraordinary things to come. "Saloon," she said again and it sounded like a blessing, or a prayer.

5

"HIYA, RAINEY!" "How you doin', honey?" "Way to go!" Laughing voices followed her as she wormed her way through the crowd packed into Doyle's bar.

"Rainey, honey," called the quarterback with the five-million-dollar hands, "you're still the prettiest yellow-haired gal I ever did see. When you going to stop this newspapering and settle down with me?"

"As soon as you learn to cook, Bubba," she hollered back.

Bubba mouthed something she couldn't quite hear, but it sounded like "hollandaise."

She plowed on. With Quinn in front of her and Kuprin and Boris shouldering through behind her, she headed for the rear of the bar—through a wedge of football players enjoying their last weeks of freedom before summer training camp opened, around a convivial clutch of basketball players, and past a dozen ex-baseball players, half of whom had known her since she was a child and still fussed over her like a troop of fond uncles. For her, Doyle's on Friday night was a boisterous Aladdin's cave—a place where remembered exploits always became more marvelous in the retelling.

Boris's improbable bulk looked almost normal in the midst of Doyle's Friday-night regulars. Kuprin preened at his reflection in the mirror over the back bar before turning to the crowd as if acknowledging an impromptu curtain call, his gracious smile inviting adulation. No one noticed him. Kuprin frowned.

"Is like I am invisible," he said, his mouth petulantly pinched, his tawny eyes forlorn. "Why am I unknown? In Russia, everyone knows Kirov and Bolshoi principal dancer. Who are these peoples?"

"Athletes," said Quinn. "Ball players, mostly. Baseball, football, basketball—they are popular American games."

"Games?" Kuprin shook his head. "Tchk!" he said dismissively.

Rainey wanted to smack him. Quinn caught her eye with a look that said, "What did you expect?" and for a moment his hand rested lightly on her back. It was the fond touch of a trainer trying to gentle a nervous filly, and she caught her breath. She loved it.

I'm doing this for the story, she reminded herself. *Quinn and I need this story.*

"What'll it be?" said Doyle, wiping down the bar in front of them.

Rainey swallowed hard and looked at Quinn again. His eyes said, "This is it." And, "Don't worry, I'm with you all the way." Then they both glanced at Doyle before allowing their eyes to linger meaningfully on Boris. They did this with such elaborate attempts at nonchalance she very nearly laughed out loud.

Doyle polished the bar in generous circles and studied Boris, his eyes flickering like a racetrack tout's estimating a horse's stamina.

"Wodka," said Kuprin. "We must drink Russian wodka. Is best wodka in world."

"You bet," said Doyle. "Coming right up."

"Why not?" said Quinn, grinning at Rainey.

"*Da!*" said Boris.

Rainey smiled at Quinn, deliberately keeping her eyes away from Doyle who was fussing over four double-shot glasses. He set the drinks before them: Rainey first, then Kuprin, next Quinn and last Boris.

Rainey raised her glass in a toast. "To a magnificent performance, Mr. Kuprin." They all touched glasses. Rainey sipped. The vodka tasted like something a trainer might rub on a sprained back. Quinn took a swallow. She knew he would rather drink beer.

Kuprin knocked back his shot, exhaled a harsh "*Hoo!*" and said, "*Boizhemoi!* Is good."

Boris sniffed as fastidiously as a teataster. "Is not good wodka, Aleksey Maximovitch. Is spoiled."

Doyle coughed.

Rainey froze.

"Spoiled?" piped Quinn on a rising note, as though his swallow had gone down the wrong pipe.

Kuprin shook his head. "How can wodka spoil, Boris Sergeyevitch? Is good wodka." And he put out his hand....

Powerless, because it was happening in an instant that had slipped the bonds of time, she watched his hand dip toward Boris's glass slowly, gracefully. His palm was square, the fingers stubby and strong, and so elastic was the moment that as he raised the glittering glass to his lips she saw that the ends of his fingers were blunt and the nails close cut with moons of extraordinary whiteness. Then time collapsed into itself, and Kuprin drank the vodka in one gulp.

"Boizhemoi!" said Quinn, his hand covering his eyes.

Rainey took a deep breath and tossed off the rest of her vodka.

"Ahhhh!" said Kuprin. The tips of his ears gleamed scarlet. "Is good. Another drink for my friend Boris Sergeyevitch, and another for me."

She threw a despairing look at Doyle.

Quinn's hands hovered at his waist, his right hand fisting his left palm, smacking the pocket of an invisible glove. Then one finger pointed down, every catcher's sign for a fastball.

Doyle, who had been chewing on a swizzle stick, spat several pieces of green plastic to the floor, flicked his eyes at Quinn and leaned across the bar to Boris.

"Hey," said Doyle, "you don't like the drink, I'll build you another. How about one of my specials, on the house? Kind of make it up to you."

Boris rubbed his nose like a retriever with a burr in his muzzle. "What is special?"

"Well . . ." Doyle began almost coyly. "It's a very powerful drink, so powerful I won't serve it to most guys. They're just not strong enough. I got it from a bartender in Marseilles."

"Strong enough? Hhhhha!" Boris thumped his chest. "I am weight-lifting champion of Dneprope-trovsk. Make drink, please."

"Here we go," said Doyle, and they all leaned forward, watching intently. He filled a tall glass with ice and grabbed a bottle from the back bar. "Good old Kentucky sour-mash bourbon is the base." As he poured a stream of golden bourbon Rainey was sure she glimpsed a clear liquid flowing into the glass from an invisible vial in his other hand. He didn't stop until the glass was nearly full of whisky. "Now, we stir." He stirred, raised the glass to eye level, and taking up another bottle poured as carefully as a chemist. "And last, we top it up by floating an inch of Pernod on top." He set the drink before Boris. "I call it a Cloud."

Boris assayed a slurping sip. "Is good," he said, nodding to Doyle who grinned at Rainey. Boris raised his glass and drained his Cloud in a single open-throated swallow. "Ahhhh!" He was grinning now. "Is decadent, but is good. Another, please, Comrade Barman."

"Sure thing," said Doyle. "If you think you can handle it."

"Boris Sergeyevitch is strong like bull," muttered Kuprin as his tawny eyes rolled up in his head like lemons in a slot machine. *"Boizhemoi!"* he murmured to himself.

"Da!" gargled Boris, his second Cloud now gone, and together they slid off their barstools and onto the floor like a couple of sacks of Crimean potatoes.

"Here we go, Champ," said Quinn. "All hands stand-to."

At a signal from Doyle, four New York Jets set their beer bottles on the bar and hulked over to Rainey, effectively screening them from everyone else in the bar.

Maytag Murray, three hundred and six pounds of defensive tackle, spoke for the quartet. "Yo, Rainey. Doyle blocked out the play for us. Which one of these bozos is going to sleep it off in the park?"

"The big one," she said.

"What about the shrimp?" said Maytag.

"Quinn and I'll put him in Doyle's car—it's out back."

"Happy to do that for you," grunted Maytag.

"I can handle him," Quinn said testily. He crouched over the sleeping Kuprin, hooked his hands in his armpits, and in one smooth motion slid him in an arc from the floor, up and over his shoulder as slickly as Fred Astaire preparing to walk off with Ginger Rogers. Rainey could only marvel as she followed him to the alley and Doyle's car.

"One more thing," said Quinn, "and we're practically home free." He lay Kuprin across the back seat and locked the door.

"More?" said Doyle with a strangled sound. "Aren't you two going to get in now and get out of here?"

"It's their driver," said Rainey. "He has to see the two of us leave. Alone."

"He's our alibi," said Quinn. "Just in case. C'mon, Champ." And she and Quinn walked arm in arm back through the bar and out onto the street. They strolled toward the front of the waiting car.

"Act natural," said Quinn out of the corner of his mouth.

"I am acting natural," she protested.

"Then why are you so stiff?"

"Because I'm petrified. Aren't you petrified?"

"Smile," urged Quinn with a ghastly grimace.

"Do you think he sees us?" she asked through clenched teeth. "It's hard to tell in the dark, *Ha! Ha! Ha!* but I think he's looking the other way."

"I'm going to wave. *Ho! Ho! Ho!*"

"*Ah, ha!* Isn't that kind of obvious?" They were beside the car now, stooping to peer inside.

"He's asleep!" sputtered Quinn. "Our alibi is asleep!" He rapped a couple of measures of reggae on the roof, and the driver's eyes popped wide.

"*Arrivederci!*" shouted Quinn, and together they executed a smart about-face, quick-marched down the length of the block, turned the corner in perfect unison and ran as fast as they could to the alley and Doyle's car.

"Are we being followed?" she gasped as they pounded down the alley, their footfalls loud as pistol shots.

Quinn twisted around as they ran. "I don't see anyone."

"You don't expect to see them, do you? They wouldn't be very good if you could see them."

"There's no one," Quinn assured her. He unlocked the car.

"He's still here," she said, peering into the back seat. "Still out cold. Sleeping like a baby. Let's go, Quinn, let's get out of here."

Quinn fiddled with the ignition and the engine thrummed confidently, but they didn't move.

"Is something wrong?" she asked nervously, peering all around them. "Do you see something I don't see?"

"I've never been to Maureen's. I don't know where she lives."

"In Grammercy Park. On Eighteenth between Irving Place and Third Avenue."

As Quinn nosed the sedan into the stream of oncoming traffic and headed south, she let out a long, slow sigh. She felt as though she'd been holding her breath for twenty-four hours. "Whooo-*eee!*" She slapped the dashboard. "We're almost there, Quinn. We're almost home free."

"Don't count your chickens, Champ." He gave her knee a cautionary pat, and his hand was so warm, his touch so electric that her whole leg trembled. It rattled like an aspen in a high wind.

She crossed her legs and leaned forward to flip on the radio. "Nice car," she said, still trying to control her wayward leg. She spun the dial and there was Stevie Wonder singing "We Can Work It Out," *Stevie*, she thought, *don't tempt me.* "Would you want a car like this?" she said nervously. "I wouldn't want a car like this. A Mercedes like this is all right if you're Doyle's age and you have a family and all that. I wouldn't keep a car in Manhattan, myself. But if I had to choose, if I really had my pick of any car in the world, I'd take a Lotus." Her leg stopped twitching just as she ran out of breath. "That's the house," she said. "The one with the great iron railings. Maureen has the ground floor."

Quinn whistled through his teeth. "I hate to tell you this, but we have a problem here."

She looked around frantically. "Are we being followed? Is someone behind us?" She couldn't see anything suspicious.

"Champ," said Quinn with a sigh. "There's no place to park."

"SHHH!"

"I'm not making any noise," Quinn protested.

Kuprin hung between them, his toes just off the ground, and looking, she hoped, like any drunk being carried home to bed by his friends. After prowling the neighborhood for what seemed like hours, Quinn had finally spotted a parking place on Seventeenth. They cut through an alleyway between two buildings.

"Someone's watching." She pointed to a darkened window.

"No, they're not."

"I saw that curtain twitch."

"It's only the wind."

"Hold the door." She was so nervous she nearly dropped the keys. "Quick! Inside." She didn't turn on a light until she'd thrown all the bolts and hooked the chain. When she hit the main switch, Quinn, who had been holding Kuprin in his arms, was so startled he nearly dropped him.

Mo's apartment seemed not to be a place where someone lived, but an artfully arranged series of controlled spaces. Spaces of such challenging purity they might have been an exhibit at the Museum of Modern Art. The walls were the warm, creamy white of heavy satin, the floors an ebony-stained parquet, the precise arrangement of armchairs and couch around a glass coffee table was the color of mushroom bisque. A single painting—white on white, by an artist Rainey knew was important, but whose name she could never remember—filled the wall opposite the windows. In the windows stood the only addition to the apartment that was nongeometric. A lavish Boston fern.

Quinn let out a long, slow whistle. "There's so much good taste here I can hardly stand it. I mean, what is Mo trying to prove, less is less?"

"Mo gets terribly carried away sometimes. She had this big, big thing last year for a minimalist decorator. I didn't think she'd ever get over it. Then one day she bought that fern, and I knew she was going to be all right."

Kuprin's head bobbled as he snored against Quinn's chest. "Where do you want him?" said Quinn.

"Put him in the guest room at the end of the hall. I'll take Mo's room, and you can use that couch."

"Let him have the couch. He's a good foot shorter than I am. I'll hang over the end—it's a lot shorter than your couch. I had frostbite once up in a combe on Mt. Everest, and I have to keep my feet warm. I can't let them hang out all night, they'll fall off."

"That," she said, pointing to the snoring Kuprin, "that is one of the greatest dancers in the world. If you believe the ballet's publicity handout at face value, he *is* the greatest dancer in the world. We are not going to deliver our blue-ribbon exclusive with his feet turning blue and chilblain on his precious toes. This way," she said, turning from the room.

"You're a hard woman, Archer," he muttered as he followed her down the hall and deposited Kuprin on the bed.

"He looks so . . . peaceful," said Rainey with an ill-suppressed giggle.

"Subdued," suggested Quinn.

"He's really out cold, isn't he?"

"DEFECTING DANCER DOZES," said Quinn with a satisfied chuckle.

They stood beside the bed, staring down at Kuprin. Quinn slipped off Kuprin's shoes and opened his belt.

"We did it," she said softly. "I think it just hit me. We really pulled it off. We've got him, and nobody else in the world knows where he is."

"He's ours, Champ. All ours."

"Aw *right!*" she said, raising her hand.

"Aw *right!*" Grinning, he gave her a high five.

Kuprin mewed in his sleep.

Quinn laughed and grabbed her hand. "Let's get out of here. And let him sleep it off. This calls for a celebration. Do you think your friend Mo has any champagne?"

"Mo," she said grandly, "has everything. Just follow me." Skipping with excitement she raced to the kitchen.

Quinn caught her in the doorway, picked her up at the waist and whirled her in circles, singing, "We *reee*-ly did it! We pulled it off! *Weee*'ve got him! And you were marvelous." His eyes glittered with delight. "By the time you finished with Peters he would have given you Kuprin on a platter."

"But the way you, oh, so casually suggested one location after another and kept shooting pictures like a madman—Quinn, you were fabulous. And then in the bar, I thought Doyle was absolutely paralyzed until you gave him the high sign."

"It was the way you waved at the driver that nearly broke me up. *Oooooh*," he sang out as he whirled her around and around. "You were marvelous!"

She threw back her head and laughed with delight. "*Sooooo* were you. Put me down, Quinn. I'm getting dizzy."

He set her on her feet, his eyes shining with excitement. Then he kissed her—lightly, joyfully, his lips full and tender.

"Oh!" she said, startled, pleased and confused, all at the same time.

"Rainey," he said hoarsely.

"That's okay, I didn't mind." Mind? *Mind?* Who did she think she was kidding? It was mind-blowing. PHOTOG WINS KISSING TROPHY. Would he think her an idiot if she asked him to do it again? After all, she was the one who had laid down the rules. Maybe the time had come to rewrite the rule book. Through her head danced Ernie Banks's legendary line, "It's a beautiful day—let's play two."

"I…" he began and faltered. He didn't seem to know what to do with his hands. He plunged them deep into his trouser pockets, then pulled them out only to shove them in again.

"I guess I'd better get that champagne," she said.

"Yes," he said. "I guess you'd better." His voice sounded deeper than she'd ever heard it before.

She stood for a moment with her face in the fridge, hoping the cold air would cool down the flush that burned her cheeks. She held out a bottle of champagne at arm's length and didn't turn around until she heard the cork pop. Her heart raced like a sprinter's at the sound of the starting gun.

"Glasses?" said Quinn, and his smile very nearly brought her to her knees.

"Glasses." Wasn't there a statute somewhere against any mere mortal having such beautiful teeth? "Glasses? I'll have to find the proper glasses. We can't drink champagne from jelly glasses, now can we? I wonder where Mo . . ."

"They're right there," said Quinn, pointing to the shelf in front of her nose.

Into her mind popped a thought so startling she nearly dropped the glasses. "Quinn," she said, trying to sound casual, "has it occurred to you that we are probably going to be heroes?"

"I wouldn't go that far," said Quinn.

"Well, I would. You'll see. I'll bet they'll have a special box reserved just for us at the gala Tuesday night. They'll probably give us a standing ovation. They might even give us free passes for life." A shadow seemed to touch Quinn's eyes and the realization hit her like a flash of summer lightning. "But you won't be around for life, will you? In a couple of months you'll be whoosh away."

"Yes," he said and looked away. "Let's drink that toast."

"I won't drink to our success, I'm too superstitious."

"Then we'll just have to think of something else."

"I can't think of a thing." She could hardly say, "Let's drink to your kisses," or "A toast to your sexy chin."

"To us, then." Quinn stared at her, his eyes blazing. How could eyes so dark have so much fire in them?

"To us." Her palms felt sticky, and her cheeks burned.

They touched glasses, and the crystal rang with a single pure note that hummed so sweetly it made her throat ache. Quinn smiled and sipped his wine. She smiled and did the same.

"Good," he said, his eyes never leaving hers.

His mouth, moist with wine, drove her wild. She wanted to lick the cool wine from his lips. "Yes," was the best she could manage. The fire in her cheeks had spread to her chest and was creeping lower and lower with every second that passed.

He raised his glass, his eyes never leaving hers, and drained it. He pushed back his chair and came toward her.

He was so tall. Tall and lean and hard, and she wanted him. Oh, how she wanted him. Wanted as she had never wanted any man in her life. She rose to meet him. This is crazy, she told herself. Don't be a fool. Before you know it, he'll be gone. They'll send him to Belfast, or Tokyo, and all you'll have left is some great memories and a heart full of pain.

"Let's take the wine into the garden," she said, stalling for time. "Mo has a beautiful walled garden. She even has a tree."

In one step he closed the distance between them. "Quinn," she began as his big hands tightened on her waist. "We have to talk." She could feel the tips of his fingers pressing hotly against her spine, his thumbs afire against her ribs. They had to talk, but she knew she couldn't talk here, not in the kitchen where he could see her face, where he could read the hunger in her eyes. She spun out of his grasp. "It's right through this door. The garden." She fumbled with the lock and fled into the garden where the darkness would hide her embarrassment and her longing.

After the brightness of the kitchen, it was so dark in the garden she could see nothing but vague shapes. She heard ivy rustling on walls she could not see, smelled late summer roses. Quinn came up behind her, a warm, electric presence at her back. She headed for the plum tree in the center of the garden, the beckoning umbrella of its leaves silhouetted against the city-pink sky. The welcoming shadow beneath it seemed impenetrably black and she sank into it gratefully. She sat on the cool ground and leaned against the trunk, pressing her cool wineglass against her burning cheek.

Quinn sat beside her in the darkness. "You can't run away from this," he said. "Talking isn't going to help."

It had to help. She lived by the word, didn't she?

"We were meant to be together," he said softly. "And you know it as well as I do. I've wanted you ever since I first saw you in that coffee shop in Bloomington. I wasn't sure who you were when I came up to your table, but I said to myself, if that girl isn't Rainey

Archer, I've just lost my job, because whoever she is I'll follow her anywhere."

"But Quinn, you know I don't have room in my life for you."

"It wouldn't be so hard to make room."

"Even if I did have room, the last thing I need in my life is a traveling man—a man with wings on his heels. I'm trying so hard to be sensible. What can we have when any day now you'll be gone?"

"This," he said, covering her mouth with his. His breath was hot, his tongue urgent.

She understood all too well the feelings crashing and colliding inside her—she had never wanted any man as desperately as she wanted Quinn. She knew it could never work out, that it would never last. That they were doomed to be parted almost before they could come together, and at the same time she knew a man like Quinn came along once in a lifetime—if she were lucky. And luck wasn't something she'd had all that much of.

This was no time to ask what kind of future they could have, knowing that he would leave like someone stepping off into the sky. She had seen a painting once of a room with an open door, a door that opened straight out onto the sky—a blue sky with tidy white clouds—no earth, no path to lie firmly beneath the feet, just clouds. Nothing. A universe of echoless Nothing. That was how it would be when Quinn left. He would walk through that door and be gone from her forever. And she would have a forever of Nothing.

She knew it, and she didn't care. Her need for him was stronger than her fear of pain.

"Drink this," she said pressing her glass to his mouth. Then she licked the wine from his lips and lost herself in his kisses.

She ached for the touch of his strong hand gliding over her naked body, ached for the weight of him pressing against her willing flesh, ached to cling to him, enfold him with all her strength as he thrust deep within her. She slid her hands up and over the hard muscles of his chest as his tongue urged its own desperate need and hers answered. She plunged her hands into his coarse black hair, pressing his mouth even more tightly against her own. Her body melted into his as he slid his thigh between hers, his hands pressing her against him until she could feel him hard against her.

He kissed her throat, her hair, her ears, his breath hot with longing. Her heart pounded as she circled his ear with her tongue, trailing kisses down his cheek until at last she bit his chin, and it was just as she thought it would be, and the sharpness of the bristles prickling her tongue drove her wild with desire.

They were beyond words now, their kisses and their hands spoke for them. Their clothes disappeared into the sheltering dark, then his lips were at her breast and she felt her insides blossom into a burning, flame-colored flower, and she moaned with pleasure. A new feeling possessed her. She felt wild and free. And for the first time in her life she knew she was free to be herself in a man's arms. She knew that he would be excited, not threatened, if she honestly matched his desire with her own.

"I need you," he said. "Need you. Need you. Need you," he repeated rhythmically as their bodies slid frictionless, straining flesh against flesh and he entered her fiercely, hotly, a moan rumbling in his chest matching the strong slow movements of his hips. She answered him, locking her legs around him with all her strength, the flaming petals within her darkening and convulsing as she tightened around him.

And in the last moment before she lost consciousness of everything, she thought, this is how people were meant to come together—wildly, passionately, beneath the smiling sky.

WHEN SHE CAME BACK to herself she found she was wrapped in Quinn's arms, and around them both was the duvet from Mo's bed. Quinn stirred in the darkness and kissed her hair. This, she thought, was where the story should end with, "And they lived happily ever after." But this was not an ending, and it wasn't a beginning. Their beginning would start on Monday morning when they handed Kuprin over. Until then they might as well be living in a world of suspended time in an enchanted garden.

Quinn nuzzled her hair, pressing her head against his shoulder. "Are you cold? Do you want to go in?" His lips brushed her ear.

"I like it here. With you. And the sun won't be up for hours."

His legs, which were tangled with hers, stretched out as he rolled against her. She stroked his calf with her foot.

"I think," he murmured, nibbling on her earlobe, "it's time to teach you how you make love, Peruvian style."

One by one, she bumped her fingers down the bones of his spine. When she reached the last one she said, "I thought you had to have a hammock."

"Where did you get that idea?"

"From something you said on the plane."

"You can't hold me responsible for anything I said on that plane. I wanted you so much my hands were shaking. I could hardly hold my beer, I was afraid I'd crush the can without even noticing and you'd think I was some kind of monster. Then you dropped that magazine, I kissed you before I knew what I was doing. I thought, that's done it. Now she'll call the stewardess and have me thrown off the plane, or something."

"Oh, Quinn. And I thought you were just trying to take my mind off flying."

He hugged her, and she could feel him chuckling silently.

"Will you tell me something honestly?" She kissed his shoulder.

He nuzzled her hair again. "I could never be dishonest with you."

"Have you been seriously looking for an apartment?"

"Desperately. Keeping my hands off you all this time has been the hardest thing I've ever done in my life. It ranks right up there with hanging from a helicopter in a bos'n's chair for a shot of Victoria Falls."

"That hard? I'd no idea."

"You must have had an inkling." He spoke with his lips against hers.

"Oh, Quinn, it drove me crazy every night knowing you were only inches away, on the other side of my bedroom wall. You can't guess how many nights I've wanted to sneak out to you in the darkness and slide under your sheet with you. Sometimes I'd even press my ear against the wall and hold my breath, and then I could hear you stirring in your sleep. I think you must dream a lot."

"I've been dreaming of you. It's been pure hell every morning to pass your door on the way to the shower. A couple of times I even reached for the knob."

"It was locked," she confessed.

"I know."

"If you'd knocked, I'd have opened it."

He was silent for a long time then he said, with heart-wrenching simplicity, "Sweet Rainey. Sweet,

sweet Rainey." Tenderly he brushed her lips with his own. "It's hard for me to say this...."

"You don't have to say anything, you know."

"But I do. I want you to understand.... Emotionally, I was still such a kid when I married, I was so full of ideals—foolish romantic notions about devotion and commitment. Then I went into the Navy, and when I got out I discovered that my wife... Well, you can guess what I discovered. I don't have to draw pictures."

"My poor darling," she murmured, caressing his cheek. Her heart ached for him.

"You are the only woman...I...I've wanted you so much, and I've been so afraid of being burned again. I know men aren't ever supposed to admit they're afraid, and being afraid of a relationship with a beautiful woman is probably the worst, but you show me a man who says he's never been afraid, and I'll show you a liar."

She clung to him, comforted him as she might a gallant, battle-scarred warrior. "I understand, my darling. I do understand."

He kissed her hungrily, as hungrily as a returning warrior. "Let me take you to Peru."

She nibbled on his chin. "Are you sure we don't need a hammock?"

"Just imagination," he answered as his hands closed on her breasts. "Think of mountains, think of great altitudes and cold, clean air."

But when the moment came, she felt like a diver falling backward from a boat into the sea. Quinn's weight bore her down, and she pitched backward into love.

6

RAINEY FLOATED up through a sea of sleep, her limbs as loose as sea wrack. She stretched her legs till her hips pulled taut and tried to remember the last time she'd slept so soundly. Had she been a cat, she thought, she'd be purring. She flung out a languid arm and touched not the wall beside her bed but *flesh!* Very warm flesh! Then it all came back. Quinn in the kitchen, Quinn in the garden, Quinn in the bed. She opened her eyes to look at him. He slept profoundly, sprawled on the bed as though flung down from a great height. She studied the complicated pattern of black hair on his chest, tracing concentric whorls with her fingers. "Oh, damn!" she whispered as she kissed his rising chest. Falling in love with Quinn was as hopeless as falling in love with a married man, for Quinn was married to far, far places with names she couldn't even spell.

Of course it was always possible that what she felt for Quinn wasn't love at all. Why should she jump to conclusions and assume it was love? Just because she turned all wonky inside when he looked at her and his lightest touch left her breathless, and even her toes tingled when he kissed her, and she so wanted to be near him always she would have rejoiced to awaken and find that somehow in the night they'd been joined at the hip. After all, what experience did she have of love? She'd never before felt for anyone what she felt for Quinn. But what did that prove? Probably nothing more than her own inexperience. And what about the way he made her feel when he made love to her? What did that mean? It meant she loved him. It all meant she loved him. She loved his sleeping ears, his wide happy mouth, his surprising hands, his astonishing body.

She loved every betraying inch of him. Overwhelmed by a dragging sense of loss, of his certain betrayal to come, she rolled away from him and pulled the pillow over her head to shut out the light and the sound of his breathing. She imagined her life a year from now, imagined how it would be looking back on her time with Quinn, and saying, probably to Mo, "Oh, sure, I remember that movie—I saw it with Quinn a month before he left for China." Or, "You'll love the Hen House, Quinn and I had fried chicken there a week before he left for Katmandu." Everything would date backward, measured from his certain leaving. Perhaps she could try pretending he was something other than what he was. A traveling salesman? Why not a troubleshooter for IBM who would return with ribald stories of his adventures in Albuquerque? Or, a sailor who would roll down the gangplank with a parrot on his shoulder and a gold ring in his ear? But every salesman returns to his home office, and every sailor has a home port. And she was no good at pretending.

"Oh, Quinn," she whispered into the pillow. "Why do you have to go?"

The mattress heaved, the pillow was pushed back, and Quinn curled himself around her back. "Good morning," he murmured, his mouth against her ear, and as he hugged her against him she was overwhelmed by the conviction that this was what true closeness was supposed to be—to make love, to waken, to feel so a part of another—this was what intimacy was meant to be. That they could have moments of such perfection and that Quinn would so willingly trade them for Tahiti or Tombouctou, made her want to cry out against all the generations of roaming men for whom a hearth was but a way station.

Furious, she slid out of his arms and sat up. "Why can't you be a traveling salesman?" she demanded. "Or a sailor?"

"A sailor?" he said sleepily.

"I wouldn't mind you being a sailor, really I wouldn't. I'd stand on the pier and wave goodbye. I'd even throw colored streamers in the water as your ship cast off. Then I'd count the days until I could wait at the bottom of the gangplank."

"Streamers?"

"Why not? Rainey Archer, Sweetheart of the Fleet. Damn you, Quinn. Why *do* you have to go?"

"I'm not going anywhere—except possibly into the other room to check on our Soviet Sleeping Beauty."

"I don't mean now, I mean…after. After this story has gotten you your foreign bureau, and you've finished paying off your alimony. After that. Why do you have to go back to taking pictures of jungles and deserts and all that?"

His eyes went flat and hard. "Would you give up your dream of writing about baseball to live in the bush and write about gnus?"

"Not unless you knew a gnu who could play third base. Oh, Quinn," she said, exasperated. "I thought Romeo and Juliet were supposed to be the last of the star-crossed lovers."

He pulled her back down into his arms and kissed her. "Are we perfect together?" His hands slid down her back.

"You know we are." She pressed herself more tightly against him.

"Then forget about the future. They're not going to ship me out tomorrow. No matter how good our story is, I still have to wait for an opening. It could be weeks or even months. Why not make the most of the time we do have together? Today, now, this moment is all we need to think about—let the future take care of itself."

"La di da!" she sang, pushing him away. "Gather ye rosebuds while ye may. Is that what you mean?"

"Hmm." He pulled her back and nuzzled her shoulder, and his clever hands slid along her thighs.

"How like a man! You're incorrigible, Quinn." She closed her eyes and answered his eager kisses.

"*So!*" barked a voice from the doorway. "You are beds together."

Rainey yelped, pulled the sheet up to her chin and opened her eyes in time to see Kuprin striding toward the foot of the bed, his eyes flashing.

"Is two days since I have woman. Already I am tints."

"Tints?" she all but shrieked.

"Tense," suggested Quinn.

Kuprin opened his belt. "Let us make party."

"*No!*" they shouted simultaneously. She clung to Quinn.

"Monday you will have woman," said Quinn firmly. "The day after tomorrow."

Kuprin melted onto the end of the bed, arranging himself as languidly as an odalisque. "Okay." He yawned mightily. "Why such sleep?"

"I'm awfully sorry about that," said Rainey. "But you drank Boris's drink by mistake. It was drugged."

"Ahhh." He nodded and yawned again, comprehension dawning. "And I am free man? I can be now rich American dancer?"

"Monday morning," said Rainey. "At nine o'clock we'll take you to the proper authorities."

"And where is Boris Sergeyevitch?" His eyes glinted evilly. "Did you kill him?"

"No," said Quinn emphatically. "We certainly did not kill him."

"It's my guess," said Rainey, "that right about now he's trying to explain to your ambassador just how he lost you."

"Where is this place?" said Kuprin to Quinn. "Is safe here? Is your place?"

"The apartment belongs to a friend of Rainey's, and it's perfectly safe. Believe me, no one knows you're here. No one."

"Hmmnym." Such a curious smile lit Kuprin's face, he might have been composing unprintable limericks in his head. He laughed nastily, stretched, yawned twice and fell asleep.

"Quinn!" she gasped. "The news. We forgot about the news. Quick, turn on the radio."

Quinn plucked the clock radio from the nightstand and set it on his stomach.

"We must be on the news," she said. "I'll bet the whole country is trying to figure out what happened to him."

He spun the dial from one all-news station to another, but there was nothing about a disappearing Russian dancer.

"They're hushing it up," she said. "They're hushing it up because they don't want anyone to know."

"Yet," he added ominously. "Just wait until it all hits the fan. I've been thinking about our position in this, and I think we'd be smart to call Wolfe and cut him in."

"Oh, no," she protested. "This is our story. Our exclusive. Trust me, Quinn. They're probably waiting to break the story on the evening news."

They raided Mo's freezer for a pizza and waited nervously for the next television newscast. Rainey picked off all the anchovies on her half and draped them over Quinn's half. But there was nothing on the evening news, nothing on the midnight news. It was baffling, they agreed, but a relief. Kuprin slept on while they talked and talked and talked. They compared tales of growing up, recounted their dreams, whispered their fantasies. They made love, and safe in each other's arms, they shared their secrets, breathless with wonder. They drowsed and woke to love and whispered words.

It was nearly dawn when, sliding her cupped hand over his perfect right bun, she discovered a thin crescent-shaped ridge. "What's this?" she said, tracing the line with her fingers.

"Nothing," came the muffled reply. Quinn lay on his stomach, his face buried in a pillow.

"It can't be nothing—it feels like a scar. Is this a scar? How did you get a scar here?"

"It's a birthmark."

"Let me see."

"C'mon, Rainey."

"Darling, let me see." And before he could roll onto his back she scooted over and sat on the backs of his legs. "It is a scar. A scar with teeth marks. Quinn, who or what sank such tee-tiny teeth into your beautiful bun? Out with it, tell me the truth."

"Did I tell you I did underwater photography in the Navy?"

"Very hush-hush, you said."

"Well, one day my partner and I wrapped up our shoot with a good twenty minutes on our clock, so we were just nosing around down there, enjoying the fish and the coral, when I started fooling around with a moray eel who didn't particularly want his picture taken so he decided to have me for lunch."

"What did you do?"

"Killed it, of course. Cookie broiled it with soy sauce, Japanese style, and served it to the mess for dinner."

On the back of his shoulder she found tiny pale dots, like a sprinkling of freckles, but too perfectly round to be freckles. "Are these scars, too?"

"My Mayan merit badges."

She kissed them one by one. "How, Quinn?"

"I was shooting the ruins of Tikal, in Guatemala, and wandering around in the jungle, rather aimlessly—the way you do when you have the feeling you might be about to stumble on something, but you don't know what—"

"A premonition?"

"Something like that. All of a sudden I heard this great whoomp and thrashing in the undergrowth and I thought, oh, boy, this is it, it's a jaguar. The only place to meet a jaguar is in the zoo. If you meet a jaguar in the jungle it means you've bought the farm. So I did my patented world-class broad-jump—thirty meters from a standing start, and I came down right on the edge of some farmer's secret marijuana patch.

I hit the turf just when the farmer popped out from behind a tree to find out what all the fuss was about. He had a face like a tractor tread and a shotgun with two long evil-looking barrels."

"I never dreamed photography could be so dangerous." She was aghast, but thrilled. She licked her lips. "Then what happened?"

"I tried a friendly wave and an *Adios, amigo*, to let him know I was just passing through, but he gave me this funny grin—as though he was one brick short of a full load—and decided to speed me on my way by ventilating my shoulder with a little buckshot." He stroked her side lovingly and said, "I'm glad you don't have any scars."

"But I do."

"Where?" He looked her over carefully, everywhere. He lifted her arms to stroke his thumb over her armpits, he scrutinized the nape of her neck, he examined her kneecaps and the soles of her feet, and everywhere he peered he left kisses behind. "Nothing but perfection."

"Here," she said, her finger on the underside of her chin. "Don't you see the scar?"

He tipped up her chin, then kissed the spot. "No."

"It's there. That's where I got it when Mo threw her bat during a lunchtime baseball game when we were twelve."

"Where were you?"

"Sitting on the grass behind the batter's box. Mary Pat pitched a lazy slow ball, and Mo swung so hard the bat flew out of her hand and smack into my jaw. It made a sound like a solid home run. I'd been eating Raisinets and leaned forward and waggled my jaw—just to see if it still worked—and all the Raisinets fell out. Mo saw chocolate raisins dropping on the grass and fainted dead away halfway to first base. She thought she'd knocked out all my teeth. She was thrown out at first."

Quinn stroked her hair back from her forehead. "I thought real ball players ate Milk Duds."

She snuggled against him. "What's so great about Milk Duds? I'll bet your favorite Popsicle was banana."

"How did you know that?"

She kissed his shoulder. "A woman understands these things."

"Would you like some ice cream? Wouldn't some ice cream be really great right now?"

"Is decadent, darling, but is good." How could she not love a man who suggested ice cream at four in the morning? Poor Mo, she thought. The only thing she ever gets at four in the morning is champagne. "Do you want me to look in the freezer? Mo's almost always got ice cream."

"I'll go," he said. "You stay where you are."

She straightened the bed, plumped the pillows, pulled up the sheet, ran combing fingers through her hair, and leaned back to think about Quinn's scars. They only made the rest of him more perfect. And the offhand way he relished danger excited her in ways that astonished her.

In a moment he strode in carrying a quart of Häagen-Dazs chocolate-fudge and two spoons.

"Quick," she said, pulling back the sheet. "Get in." At first they ate silently, then she sighed. "It's luscious."

"Hmmm!" He licked his lips.

"Hmmm!"

"Good!" he said.

"Oh, good."

"Oh, yes," he said. "Yes."

"Chocolate's so . . . so . . . wonnn-derful, yes."

"Yes. Yes. Yes."

"Hmm-mm!" she said breathlessly.

"Hmm-mm!" he answered with a groan.

"Oh, Quinn! That was delicious." She closed her eyes and collapsed amongst the pillows.

"I'm glad it was good for you, too," he said. She could hear his spoon scraping the bottom of the carton.

IN THE MORNING, the smell of coffee and frying bacon drew Kuprin to the kitchen. After an enormous breakfast and a two-hour shower he proclaimed himself ready to be interviewed.

Rainey settled herself in a chair across from Kuprin who arranged his limbs on the couch with a dancer's studied casualness. Behind her she heard Quinn, snapping off pictures. Kuprin lifted his chin artfully, licked his lips and turned to Quinn's lens with a dancer's eloquent gesture. Prepared to frame her questions with a diplomat's care, Rainey opened her notebook. Kuprin's tawny eyes shortened their focus to gaze into hers.

"It's understood," she began, "that the question uppermost in everyone's mind will be, 'Why did you decide to defect?'"

"Many reasons." He smiled brilliantly. Quinn's flash blazed. "I want better roles. That first importance. I not dance so often for Kirov."

"But aren't you, I mean weren't you a principal soloist with the Kirov?"

"Hmmnym." He made his running engine sound. "Sometimes yes. Sometimes no."

What is that supposed to mean? she wrote in her notebook.

"In America I will dance principal role every night. In America all girls in company will love me. Audiences will love me. Critics will love me. Everyone will love me. I will go to Hollywood make movies like Misha." Rising, he spread his arms wide, enthusiasm launching him into the air. "And I will have . . . I will have . . ." His heels beat a flamenco tattoo on the parquet. "I will have . . . credit cards!" he shouted and flung his arms toward the ceiling, his fingers popping like castanets. "American Express! Visa! Diner's Club! MasterCard!" He whirled in delirious circles, his heels exploding like firecrackers.

"*Olé!*" shouted Quinn.

Kuprin subsided, panting, onto the couch. "I will have big car, big bed, big womans."

"Big head," muttered Quinn.

"Now I have another shower," said Kuprin. "Your water so hot I could make tea."

Rainey waited until she heard the bathroom door close, then she said, "DANCER DEFECTS FOR GOLD CARD CREDIT LINE. What happened to ideals, to that passionate longing for artistic freedom? He sounds like a contestant on a mad network executive's new game show, *Defecting for Dollars*."

"It takes all kinds, Champ, darling. If you think about it, they can't all be physicists willing to starve to death for their principles. Some of them must be just like greedy people anywhere."

"What did you say?"

"The world is full of greedy people."

"I mean before that. What did you call me?"

Quinn looked puzzled. "Champ, darling?"

Her heart flopped over. "Oh, Quinn. Oh, darling."

He crossed the room in three strides and pulled her down on the couch. "What is it?"

"You never called me 'darling' before. Kiss me, before I do something violent, like tear off your shirt."

His mouth covered hers, and he pressed her down on the couch.

"What are you doing?" she said.

"You know what I'm doing."

"But we can't. Not now. Not here with him in the shower."

"Sure we can. He won't be out till the water runs out." He spoke with mouth against hers. "What d'ya say, Champ, darling?"

"Is decadent, darling, but is good."

"Is THERE any coffee left?" asked Quinn, putting his head around the swinging door that divided the kitchen from the pantry. "What are you doing?"

"Washing lettuce. There's some still hot in the pot. I thought I'd make tuna fish salad for lunch. Is that okay?"

"With chopped egg in it?"

"Sure, if you want."

"And lots of mustard?"

"Do you want to make it?"

"You make great tuna salad. Ilga never made tuna salad." He set his coffee cup on the table and came up behind her at the sink to take her head in his hands and part her hair on her neck as though he were preparing to braid it into pigtails. So unexpectedly revealed, the nape of her neck felt chilled and vulnerable. She shivered slightly as he bumped his thumb down her astonished neck bones. Then he kissed them, one by one, until he reached her collar. There he stopped, sighed a deep, satisfied sigh, and lifting her hair as he might a curtain, replaced it on her neck and stepped away.

The entire action took no more than ten seconds, and yet in that brief span she knew such sweet pleasure her heart seemed to expand between beats and her veins run with honey. When she turned around, he was gone.

She wondered if this was a foretaste of what it would be like. A sweet goodbye, and he'd be gone in a puff of smoke.

She piled the last of the lettuce in the salad basket and carried it into the bright garden to shake off the excess water. Smiling to herself she walked down the flagged path to Mo's plum tree. It was her plum tree now, hers and Quinn's. She touched the sun-warmed bark and a shiver of memory ran through her. Here, beneath this tree, hidden from the hundreds of windows that overlooked the garden, they'd made such glorious love, shared such intimacies. No man had ever been as open, as unashamedly honest with her as Quinn had been in the sheltering dark—and since. She had never imagined that there were men of such infinite tenderness and warmth.

They had made a pact not to plan beyond tomorrow. To take each day as it came and treasure each other for the time they had. Women, she knew, had been making this same bargain since the beginning of time. *Why,* she wondered, *does it always seem harder for the woman than the man? Is it because we know what the last chapter will be, while men, who are so much more romantic than we, like to think they can rewrite the book?*

In the cool kitchen she spread the lettuce on a towel, rolled it and put it in the fridge. She put two eggs on to boil.

Not so many hours ago Quinn had said to her, "You're so different from Ilga." They had devoured all the ice cream and exchanged cold, chocolate kisses. "You're so passionate, so giving. Lovemaking for Ilga was like an Olympic event. I guess that goes with being a gymnastics coach."

"I thought you said she ran a cooking school."

"She does. Now. She coached gymnastics until she got fat. Well, not fat exactly, but hefty. Hefty for a gymnastics coach. As things turned out, it was a good thing in the end, because when she fell off the balance beam she didn't hurt herself, she bounced down the mat like a medicine ball. It was after the fall that she took it up. Cooking. Serious cooking."

Poor Ilga, she thought. Had she taken refuge in food when she saw the end was coming? Would she?

"But is stunning collection," Kuprin was saying when she went into the living room to call them for lunch.

"Kuprin admires your friend's video tape library," said Quinn, holding her chair for her. "Particularly the old movies."

"Is remarkable," Kuprin marveled. "I must have one. And VCR, also. Big television is first thing I will buy. I would like see film, please, after luncheon."

"Anything you want," said Rainey. "But right now, I think we should talk about our plan for Monday morning."

"The point of this scheme," explained Quinn, "is to be as inconspicuous as possible. At eight-forty precisely I will bring the car up this street. You and Rainey will be watching from the window. When you see me enter the street you will leave the apartment and walk casually to the front door of the building. As you open the door I will drive to the curb. You and Rainey will jump in, and we'll drive over to Federal Plaza."

"That's where Immigration is," added Rainey.

"*Da!*" said Kuprin with a solemn nod.

"Quinn will park in the cabstand," Rainey continued. "And then we'll stroll into the building just like any three people going about their business. Okay?"

"Hhhokay."

"Now," said Rainey. "What movie would you like to watch?"

"*The Red Shoes,*" said Kuprin.

"But why?" said Kuprin, knuckling the tears from his eyes. "Explain, please."

Rainey blew her nose. "I can't." The ethereal Moira Shearer, the exquisite ballerina with the flaming red hair, married the man she loved—the composer-conductor with the beseeching eyes and supplicating hands—but she couldn't have both marriage and dancing, though why, exactly, Rainey couldn't quite figure out. What was terribly clear was that Moira

Shearer, unable to resolve her conflict, took Anna Karenina's way out and threw herself in the path of an oncoming train.

"But many ballerinas marry," said Kuprin. "Have babies. They come back, dance again. Makarova. Makarova have baby. Is very puzzling."

Quinn, who had been silent, said, "You have to understand that *The Red Shoes* was made a long time ago. It's a very old-fashioned movie. It expressed the sensibility of another time. Women's lives are different now. Their expectations have changed." He stared at his hands, then looked up at Rainey. "You wouldn't let yourself be caught in a trap like that, would you?"

"I wouldn't see it as a trap," she said, and even as she spoke she knew she was inching out on a high and lonely branch. "I think a marriage has to be . . . well, I know it sounds dumb, but I think a marriage should be elastic, stretchable—sort of like a dancer's tights."

Quinn, who had been studying his hands again, looked up.

She pictured herself reaching out to grasp a saw. "A marriage," she said, starting in on the branch, "should give enough to contain anything you want to put into it—two careers, six kids, whatever."

"And if it doesn't?" said Quinn.

"Then it's not a marriage." She'd sawed the limb clean through.

7

AFTER DINING on steaks, which she filched from Mo's freezer and Quinn barbecued to perfection on a hibachi in the garden, she opened her notebook again while Kuprin described his training at the Vaganova School of Ballet in Leningrad.

"Is same school for Baryshnikov," he said proudly. He recounted some of the stories that floated back to the Russian ballet world about Misha and Nureyev and Makarova. His eyes shown with longing for a life like theirs. To her astonishment he seemed to know to the penny the fees and salaries they commanded.

"So he's venal?" said Quinn with a shrug. "There are worse things to be, I guess." She was loading the dishwasher and he had followed her to the kitchen for another cup of coffee.

"Name one," she said. She felt cheated. She dumped in the soap and slammed the door. "It's just that I thought he'd be so different. Above all that. I don't know." She thumped the buttons.

He took her in his arms. "Baryshnikov and those others probably are different, but he's still a good story, isn't he?"

At eleven o'clock she turned on the television, and the late news flickered over them. Nothing much seemed to be happening. It was the slow, dead-end of summer. Congress was in recess. The President was vacationing at Camp David. The Yankees were still seven games behind Boston. Nothing more than the usual skirmishes anywhere in the world. In television terms, there was no news.

The lead story was a human interest piece featuring an ex-senator from Georgia who had taught himself to play the Georgia fight song on glasses from the Senate dining room. With eight water tumblers forming an imperfect octave, he tapped out "I'm a rambling wreck from Georgia Tech," with a dessert spoon, but before he could finish the second bar, the screen went mercifully blank. The weekend anchor came on, gaping, a late bulletin rattling in his flustered hand.

"The Soviet embassy. . ."

"Oh, boy!" said Rainey.

"Here we go," said Quinn.

". . . in Washington has, this evening, demanded that a warrant be issued . . ."

"What is warrant, please?" said Kuprin.

"Shhh!" they said.

". . . for the arrest of the person or persons unknown, who kidnapped—somewhere on the streets of Manhattan, Friday night—Aleksey Maximovitch Kuprin—"

"Hhhokay!" whooped Kuprin. "Is good publicity, yes?"

"Is rotten!" said Quinn.

"—a principal dancer with the Kirov Ballet of Leningrad. The Soviet government has lodged a severe protest—"

"Severe protest?" Rainey moaned.

"Did you expect them to applaud?" said Quinn.

"—with the Secretary of State, and has termed the alleged abduction highly provocative."

"Provocative I like," beamed Kuprin. "Means sexy, yes?"

"Not in this case," said Rainey.

"…Mr. Kuprin," the announcer read, "was brought to New York by the American Ballet Studio to dance at its gala on Tuesday evening."

There followed a statement by Peters, the company public relations man, deeply regretting this tragic incident, and several photos of Kuprin, who was now pointing gleefully at the screen and bouncing up and down in his chair. Lastly, a police captain explained that the missing dancer had been touring the city in the company of two *Journal* reporters, his bodyguard, Mr. Tolinkov, and his chauffeur. The chauffeur was certain that the reporters left Mr. Kuprin and Mr. Tolinkov at a midtown drinking establishment. Mr. Tolinkov was not available for comment, nor had the police been able to locate the reporters. The public's help was requested.

The image flipped on the screen and there they were, side by side—*Journal* file photos of Quinn and her in grainy black-and-white that looked like wanted posters on a post office wall.

Quinn groaned and turned off the set as the weather map filled the screen. She sat very still, staring at the shrinking white dot of phosphorescence spinning into infinity, sucking her confidence in after it. Quinn took her hand and held it very tight. "Champ, darling," he said at last. "It's hit the fan."

"Is *good!*" Kuprin crowed. "Good! Good! Good! Is wonderful publicity. Now everyone in country know Kuprin. Gala will be all success. You, too, will be famous."

"Thank you very much," she said, laughing. "He's right, Quinn. Don't you see it? The harder they look—"

"The bigger our story," finished Quinn. A big grin split his serious face and he hugged her joyfully.

"*Boizhemoi!* I will be rich."

"This is our grand-slam home run," she chortled against Quinn's shoulder and hugged him back.

The ringing phone shattered their laughter. In unison they spun around to stare at the phone with that mixture of loathing and apprehension usually reserved for snakes.

"Don't touch it," cautioned Rainey. "Let the answering machine take it."

On the third ring the tape began spooling up the message.

"Is police," whispered Kuprin. His face was the color of wet newsprint.

The tape revolved.

"It can't be," Quinn assured him, but he caught her eye with a look that said, "Cross your fingers."

The tape stopped and the message light blinked balefully.

She hit the Playback button.

"Honey—" the voice was Mo's "—I don't know what you've gotten yourself into, but if there's anything I can do to help, you know where to find me. I'll be back in the city tomorrow."

She threw herself on Quinn's chest and all but sobbed with relief. "That was my friend," she explained to Kuprin as she gasped for breath. Quinn patted her back. "This is her apartment. She is my best friend."

"I hhhope," said Kuprin. "Where is wodka, please. I need drink."

"DO YOU WANT another slice of toast?" she asked Quinn.

"I'm not sure I could stand the noise."

"Do you have enough film?"

"Of course I have enough film. What do you take me for, a bloody amateur?"

"I was just asking. You don't have to jump down my throat."

"Who sat up all night playing nursemaid to a dancing lush?"

"He's not a lush," she insisted. "He's just nervous."

"You had to be there," groaned Quinn. "He sobbed his way through *The Red Shoes* three times and put away a quart of vodka. How did you sleep?"

"Not very well. I had a lot of funny dreams. Nervous about this morning, and Immigration and all that." That may have been the cause, but it was Quinn she had dreamed about.

In the one she remembered most clearly, Quinn, in his shorts with the whales on them, posed with one perfectly arched foot balancing on a globe that was the earth. His calf was tensely knotted, and from his heels wings sprang. Though his body was restrained by mysteriously snakelike cables, eels perhaps, he seemed to be flying through space beneath his flat soup plate of a hat that sprouted wings as well. It was only when she woke that she connected the image of Quinn with the picture of Mercury that was always on the front of the telephone book when she was a kid.

Kuprin, fresh from what Rainey guessed must be his fourteenth shower, joined them in the living room.

"Ready?" she asked. "It's time."

Kuprin nodded solemnly.

"Give me a kiss for luck," said Quinn. "And watch for the car." He snatched an all-too-brief kiss and swung out the door.

Kuprin sidled up to the window. Furtively he peered at the street through the burgeoning Boston fern. When she came up beside him, he jumped.

"It's too early," she assured him, checking her watch. "He hasn't had time to reach the car yet. It's around on the other side of this block."

"Hmmnym." He sounded skeptical. He paced from the window to the far wall and back to the window.

She fingered the fern. It felt cool. Soothing. She checked her watch again. Where was he?

Kuprin paced, his hands clasped behind his back, his head forward, his anxious eyes flicking between the parquet and the street. "Hmmnym?" he murmured. "Where is your lover?"

"Stop fidgeting," she said. "He'll be here." *My lover,* she thought. *Quinn is my lover. And I am Quinn's lover. And I can hardly believe it, even now. That fabulous man is my lover.* She stared up the street. *That fabulous man is late.*

"Something's wrong," she said aloud. It was nearly nine o'clock. "Come on, we're going to find him."

"I wait here." He cowered behind the fern.

"No you don't," she said, reaching through the leaves to pluck at his arm. "We're going together." What if they had been followed, after all? What if Boris and his friends had been waiting to pounce? What if Boris and his friends had found Quinn?

She dragged a reluctant Kuprin out the back door and raced between two buildings to the other side of the block. She heard Quinn even before she saw him. He leaned against Doyle's car, his face a mask of fury, slamming his fist against the roof and swearing like a sailor. The car hunkered on the asphalt, its wheels gone, one window smashed, the dashboard stripped. *Sid lives!* proclaimed the fluorescent message spray-painted across the side.

"Boizhemoi!" said Kuprin, his palms to his cheeks. "Is worse than KGB."

They rode to 1 Federal Plaza in a taxi with Kuprin wedged, twitching, between them. At the first stop-light the driver twisted around in his seat and said, "I'll bet you can't guess who I had in my cab last night."

"Who?" said Quinn impatiently.

"C'mon," said the cabbie. "You're not even trying. You're supposed to guess. Hey," he said to Kuprin, "you look kind of familiar. Should I know you? Are you somebody?"

"The light's green," said Rainey, before Kuprin could answer. CURIOUS CABBIE FOILS FREEDOM RIDE. "Let's go before you miss the light." Quinn reached across Kuprin's knees to take her hand. The taxi lurched forward. She squeezed Quinn's hand.

"I got it!" said the cabbie over his shoulder as he hit the brakes at Federal Plaza. "You're what's-his-name. You play second base for the Toronto Blue Jays. Right?" A fierce look from Rainey kept Kuprin silent. The cabbie appealed to Quinn. "Don't he play for Toronto?"

"Left field," said Quinn. "He's way out in left field." He paid the driver and opened the door.

"Ready, Champ?" said Quinn.

"I am, if you are." With Quinn beside her she could do anything. Anything. She smiled into his eyes and felt slightly larger than life. They were about to become heroes. JOURNAL REPORTERS BRING DANCER TO FREEDOM. HEROES FETED BY GRATEFUL DANCE WORLD.

"Kuprin, you all set?" he said.

"*Da!*"

"Then let's go get 'em!"

She and Quinn kept Kuprin between them as they crossed the sidewalk to the entrance. Her stomach churned when they entered the lobby. She admired the steadiness of her hand as she reached for the elevator button, then was mortified to see her fingers trembling. They had the elevator to themselves, and Quinn appeared completely relaxed. He leaned against the back of the elevator; only the pulse hammering at his temple betrayed his excitement. Kuprin, deathly pale, carried himself like the princely scion of some long-deposed Balkan monarchy about to assert a doubtful claim to a vanished throne.

"Window Seven," she said to Kuprin.

He grunted as the doors opened to a blinding burst of television lights and shouts of "There he is!" and "He's here!" and "Stop pushing!" Strobes popped above the heads of a hurrying crowd of reporters.

"Oh, my God!" she said.

"Hey! What's going on?" said Quinn. He grabbed Kuprin's shoulder and spun him around.

"Is welcoming committee. Just like plan."

"Plan?" she said. "What plan? Not our plan."

"Whose plan?" hissed Quinn, his eyes narrowing.

"Peters and Marion," squealed Kuprin. "And mine, also. Make media events. Is wonderfuls. *Boizhemoi!* Television everywhere. Everyone in America recognize Kuprin now. On *Live at Five* all America will watch Kuprin defect." He twisted free and rushed down the corridor and into the lights.

Quinn punched viciously at the Lobby button. "We've been had."

She was so angry she could barely speak. "Taken for a ride," she managed finally.

"Played for a couple of suckers. They set us up for this, knowing damn well you'd want to do the patriotic, all-American thing and help that sniveling twit."

"And don't think I won't say so when I write my story."

"What story? I WAS A SHILL FOR THE BALLET?"

"If you look at it sort of inside out there's still a great story here—using the press, abusing the press for their own selfish aims. I'm going to give it to all of them— in spades. There might even be a Pulitzer in all this if I can only find the right angle to sell it to Wolfe."

"And if Wolfe doesn't see it your way?"

She flung out of the building and glowered up at the sky. "Then what we have on our hands is a fiasco of truly awesome proportions."

"Rainey," he said as he wrapped her tightly in his arms, "look at me. Here's an angle for you: if it hadn't been for this Kuprin caper, we might never have gotten together."

How solid he was. How reassuring. How full of gallant baloney. She kissed his cheek. "Do you really believe that?"

"No," he rumbled.

"Neither do I."

RAINEY DUMPED HER NOTES out on her desk. "We have more than an hour's grace before Wolfe gets in. I should be able to start making sense of all this by then. Where's my tape recorder? Have you seen my tape recorder?"

Quinn patted his camera bag. "I'll run this film down to the lab and be right back."

"Arr-chur! Quinn! Now!" Wolfe's voice snarled over the empty Sports department like raging thunder.

She looked up at Quinn. "It's only nine-thirty, what's he doing here so early? He doesn't sound too happy. Do you suppose he knows already?"

Quinn touched her shoulder. "Let's go find out."

Hands brushing, they walked to Wolfe's desk. He did not ask them to sit down.

"Why?" said Wolfe. "Tell me why?" He rolled a yellow copy pencil between his palms. It clicked against his ring. "Why didn't you two numbskulls tell me what you were doing? What do you think I'm here for? Window dressing? I'm your editor, fercrissake!" His voice was hoarse, his eyes red, and his face had the mealy look of a man who'd been kept up all night.

She took a deep breath. "I was afraid you'd take me off the story and give it to Billings."

"You're greedy, the both of you. Assignments are my decision. You two work for me. For the team. You are not free agents."

"We know that," said Quinn through clenched teeth.

"Aaah!" Wolfe snapped the pencil in two and threw the pieces at the wastebasket. "Do you know what happens to rookies who don't make it in the big leagues? I'll tell you what happens to rookies—"

"Rookies?" Quinn exploded. "Who are you calling rookies? Rainey's the best sportswriter you've ever had—"

"Rookies?" She spat the word vehemently. "Quinn's pix are famous all over the world, and I've—"

"Yes, rookies." *Click-click. Click-click.* Wolfe rolled a new yellow pencil between his palms and waited. When she and Quinn fell into fuming silence he continued. "Rookies who can't cut it with the big boys are sent down to the minors. And that's where you're going. Both of you—"

"But it was my fault," she broke in. "Quinn said over and over we should call you, but—"

"It was Rainey who wanted to call you, I was the one who—"

She could have kicked him.

"Shut up!" roared Wolfe. He selected another pencil. "Archer, I've transferred you to the Life/Style section. Quinn, you're on City Hall. Starting now.

Archer, go clean out your desk. And if I ever see either one of you around my Sports department again, you'll find yourselves flying out of here faster than a slapshot."

"But we were suckered into it," she protested. "Suckered by our own publisher's wife. She used us, me. She manipulated this paper. Isn't it important to expose that? Don't you care?"

"Care? I care that reporters are supposed to think." He snapped another pencil. "Think for themselves, Archer. Ask questions. Why didn't you ask enough questions to figure it out? If you'd paid more attention to your job instead of making bedroom eyes at Quinn, here..."

"That calls for an apology," shouted Quinn, his fists balled on the desk as he loomed over Wolfe. "If you don't take that back, I swear I'll deck you."

"Aaaah, women!" said Wolfe with a dismissive wave of his pencil. "Okay. I take it back. But if you'd been a little less greedy for an exclusive, if you'd called me, the way you're supposed to, I would have figured it out for you. That's my job. Don't you yo-yos ever learn? Editors are supposed to help you think."

"Please, Wolfe," she pleaded. "Not Life/Style. I'd rather do real estate. Obits. Let me write obits. Wolfe, have a heart. Life/Style is for all those croissant nibblers. Our women readers don't eat croissants, they eat Oreos and Twinkies because that's what they buy for their kids—"

Quinn touched her arm. "Champ," he muttered softly, "there's a time to hold 'em and a time to fold 'em."

"I know," she moaned. "I know." She gave up trying to keep the hollow sound of despair out of her voice. Wolfe glared at her, and she glared back. "But what about our story? Quinn has hundreds and hundreds of pictures. There's still a terrific story here. Can't you see that? At least let us do this story before we leave."

Wolfe chewed his current pencil. He left deep chomp marks.

"Wolfe?" she said. Her hands were shaking.

He shook his head. "I had hope for you, Archer. You coulda been a contender."

"Dammit! I'm still a contender," she insisted loudly, despite Quinn's restraining hand on her arm.

"Give your notes and pix to Billings. And you'd better toe the line at Life/Style and do your job, or I promise you I will personally see to it that you never write for another paper. Anywhere. Sister, you won't even be able to get the shrimp beat in New Orleans."

"Don't call me *Sister*, you . . . you . . . You're a real rat, Wolfe."

"I know." He spoke with relish and a nasty, self-satisfied grin.

She walked with Quinn as far as the elevator before she threw herself, despairing into his arms. "I've screwed things up so."

"It's not your fault." He pressed her head against his shoulder and stroked her hair. "It's not."

"Of course it is. Don't be so damned noble. You wanted to go to Denmark, or Durban. Now you'll be lucky if they send you to Duluth. I don't know how I'm ever going to make it up to you. And I was so sure we'd both score with this one." She winced at the tears stabbing her eyes and squinched her eyes shut tight against them. Her whole body shook with the effort.

Quinn's arms tightened around her and he kissed her hair. "Didn't someone say, 'It's not over till it's over'?"

"Oh, Quinn," she gasped, half laughing half sobbing. "How about, 'It's only a game,' or, 'It ain't over till the fat lady sings'?"

8

"I WANT YOU to understand," said Edie, "I'm only putting you on my Life/Style staff as a favor to Roland."

Roland? Who was Roland? The caressing way she wrapped her tongue around Roland suggested to Rainey that there was almost nothing Edie wouldn't do for her Roland.

Edie must have read her bewilderment in her face. "Mr. Wolfe," she explained with a chiming shrug. Her zillion gold bracelets rang tunefully.

Rainey put two and two together, factored in the wife who bred schnauzers in Larchmont and came up with three—a very odd number. She studied Edie with renewed interest. Edith, née Wilmer, Lambino Rochick Morales Stewart—no one could say she hadn't kept trying—was known to every *Journal* reporter as Evil Edie. Her temper was the stuff of which newspaper legends are made. One of those legends had it that she had once used her gold Paloma Picasso ballpoint to stab a reporter through the hand because she had misspelled Gucci. Edie, who **had** the petulant mouth and resentful eyes of a beauty pageant oboist who has just lost the talent competition to a baton twirler, was in fact rumored to have been runner-up for Miss All-Aluminum Cookware in Manitowoc, Wisconsin. She had the best body that sweat and effort could buy, and thick ankles. The ankles softened Rainey's heart. Anyone with ankles like that had to have a spot of humanity buried in her somewhere.

"I don't suppose," said Edie doubtfully, "you know anything about lips."

"Lips?" She knew something about split lips. And she was learning all about Quinn's lips and hoped to learn a great deal more—pursuing her studies of Quinn's lips as diligently as any night-school student—but she didn't think Edie wanted to hear about Quinn's lips.

"My lip person is tied up on a sun-block piece. I need someone to do lip liners, lipsticks and pucker cream."

"No," she said firmly. "I don't know a thing about lips." And heaven help any woman, she prayed silently, who couldn't manage a pucker without pucker cream.

Edie raised her hands and lowered them in helpless resignation. Her bracelets clattered against the desk. "Roland," she said, invoking the magic name, "tells me you did general news and features before he took you on at Sports. I think I'll give you . . ." She rummaged through a pile of assignment sheets. "This one." She handed a sheet across the desk to Rainey.

"Cynthia Peabody," said Rainey, reading from the top of the bio.

"That's *Pee*-b'dee," said Edie sharply.

"Yes, of course," mumbled Rainey, feeling like a jerk.

Edie sniffed. "She's the Peabody of Bell, Beale, Peabody, and Hoskins. Cynthia Peabody is one of New York's leading corporation counsels. She specializes in corporate takeovers. She's married to Richard Hoskins. They have one son. I want a story on how she manages her life, how she combines marriage, family, motherhood and the law. Your angle is: superior women accomplish superior things with ease and grace. You'll interview her at her office. I want to know every last thing about how she does it, how she organizes her life. Who does her hair? How often? When? Talk to her doorman. Her secretary. Her housekeeper. Everyone. The story is for our Coping series: How to Travel in the Fast Lane. You've followed our Coping series." This was not a question, but a statement.

"No, I'm afraid I haven't." Her palms began to sweat.

Suspicion narrowed Edie's eyes. "You *have* kept up with the Life/Style section."

"I'm sorry, but Wolfe keeps, I mean, kept me pretty busy." Would Edie run her through with her cute little gold pen? Would she run Wolfe through for sending her such a dodo?

Edie bit her lip. "Then you have until your appointment tomorrow. Well, don't just sit there. Get downstairs to the library. I want you to read a year's back issues before you go home tonight. A full year. Is that understood?"

"Yes, Mrs. Stewart."

"And Archer, Life/Style reporters do not go out on interviews dressed as casually as sportswriters. I expect you to be a credit to Life/Style when you walk into Bell, Beale, Peabody, and Hoskins. Do I make myself clear?"

"Yes, Mrs. Stewart." Edie meant high heels. She hadn't had to wear heels even once since becoming a sportswriter. She hated heels. She couldn't run after a story in heels. And besides, they hurt. She saw it all in a flash: JOURNAL REPORTER SLAYS EDITOR OVER SHOE CODE. SHOE CODE SLAYER GETS LIFE.

RAINEY SLOGGED DUTIFULLY through screen after screen of microfilm back issues until she was certain her eyes had begun to cross. She looked up to see the librarian standing beside her.

"This is for you," whispered the librarian. She set a brown bag in front of Rainey.

"For me?" said Rainey. "Who's it from?"

"Shhh!" warned the librarian, a finger to her lips.

Rainey opened the bag to the scent of fresh coffee. Taped to the lid of the coffee container was a note:

Hang in there, Archer. We're rooting for you.
Jellicoe & Cuddy.

Wrapped in a napkin was a cheese Danish.

"Is anything wrong?" whispered the librarian.

Rainey could only shake her head and grin.

It was on her way back from splashing cold water on her eyes that she suddenly remembered Doyle and his car. She'd been so absorbed in her own problems that she'd completely forgotten about him. She ducked into Real Estate and grabbed the phone from an empty desk.

"Rainey, honey," said Doyle. "What happened? Did you do you-know-what with you-know-who?"

"You're never going to believe this," she began.

"Try me," he insisted, and he listened without comment to her judiciously edited account of their weekend with Kuprin and its sorry climax. It was only after he had commiserated feelingly over her loss of the perfect exclusive, that she brought up the matter of his vandalized car.

"I'll pay," she hastened to add. "Really I will."

A long silence followed—a silence as hollow and cheerless as a cave—then a sigh like the wind in a tunnel. "Sid lives?" said Doyle. "Who-the-hell is Sid?"

Back in the library, she munched her Danish, sipped her coffee and thought about Quinn. Their days together had so changed her life that after spending the weekend in his arms, try as she might, she could not imagine what her life was going to be without him. There was plenty of time to find that out when he left. Meanwhile, she wasn't going to spoil the time they had with moaning. She wasn't going to waste her time scheming to find some way to nail his feet to the floor.

Quinn was a traveling man, and nothing would ever change him. *Is that part of why I love him?* she wondered, because I can never really have him?

QUINN MET HER at the door with open arms, and she sank into them gratefully. He kissed her for about an hour, his hands chasing themselves all over her back. SPORTSWRITER FALLS FOR DEMON KISSER.

"Keep your eyes closed," he said when they came up for air. "I have a surprise."

"What surprise? Today has already had enough surprises to last me for the rest of my life. I'm surprised out."

"Eyes closed," he ordered. "Take my hand and follow me."

Of course she had to know where he was leading her; it was her apartment, after all. But eyes closed, as ordered, she followed him to the bedroom. "Now?" she said.

"Not yet."

She heard the light snap on.

"Now," said Quinn.

She stared, speechless. Her narrow twin bed had been replaced by a king-size one that filled the room from wall to wall to wall to wall. Her dresser was now behind her in the hall beside the john. "It's big," she said. "String a net across it and we could play tennis on it."

"You don't like it."

"Of course I like it. It's going to be marvelous making love on that bed...."

"But? I can hear the but in your voice."

"I was just wondering, how do I get in the closet? The door's blocked. And I don't have any sheets this big. We have to have sheets, Quinn."

"The closet?" He rubbed his chin and glowered at the closet door. "Is that all? I'll take the door off its hinges, and we'll buy sheets." He pulled her down on the bed. "Tennis, anyone?"

"I've never made love on a bare mattress," she said.

"You look great in stripes. Besides, I have. Lots of times."

"I thought you were partial to Peruvian hammocks. No—" She touched his lips. "Don't tell me about your conquests." She tangled her fingers in his hair.

"I've missed you," he murmured, his lips against her throat.

"What's that?" She heard a faint ringing.

"What's what?"

"Don't you hear a bell? I hear a bell."

"Lovely things, bells." He opened the top button of her blouse.

"It's the phone. Quinn, what did you do with the phone? Where is it?"

"The phone," said Quinn thoughtfully. He looked around him, but there was nothing to see but bed. "I think it's under that corner." He pointed to the corner nearest her right foot. "Once I have the door off," he suggested cheerfully, "you can put the phone in the closet." He snaked an arm between the bed and the wall and after some tugging handed her the phone.

"Hello?" she said as Quinn rolled to the doorway and disappeared.

"Did you watch the evening news?" It was Mo. She raced on without waiting for an answer. "I just saw the ABC footage of you and some hunk in an elevator delivering that Russian dancer to the government this morning."

Quinn was back with a screwdriver in his hand.

"I was right, wasn't I?" Mo continued. "You were hiding him at my apartment, weren't you? Did you know the whole thing was a publicity stunt? No, I don't suppose you would have done it if you had. And who was that hunk in the elevator with you?"

"You're right," she said, "I didn't know it was a stunt. And we did hide him at your apartment. I owe you a bottle of champagne and a whole bunch of steaks and stuff. And that hunk in the elevator was Quinn."

Quinn waded across the bed to apply the screwdriver to the top hinge pin on the closet door. He smacked it sharply with the heel of his hand.

"What's that funny noise?" said Mo.

"That," said Rainey, "is Quinn, who, not content to fill my bedroom with a bed the size of Yankee Stadium, is now standing on said bed, taking down my closet door."

"Bingo!" crowed Mo.

Quinn grinned down at her and started on the middle hinge pin.

Mo said, "Are you going to tell me what Aleksey Kuprin is really like, or are you going to make me wait to read all about him in your story tomorrow morning?"

"You won't be reading about him under my byline, I'm afraid. Mo, we've been busted."

"I've always said your Wolfe is a subhuman. Are you completely off the paper, or just demoted to shipping clerk?"

"Quinn's stuck down at City Hall and I've been banished to Life/Style. Did you know that you can lose ten pounds in ten days on a broccoli and rice diet? And take warning, my dear, A-line silk skirts are now out for the cocktail hour. However, balloon-tiered taffeta and anything *point d'esprit* will be in for party dresses this fall."

"*Point d'esprit?* Rainey, you must be cracking up. Quit before your brain turns to radiccio. You don't belong there. Resign, and come work for me."

She shook her head. "I'm not going to let Wolfe beat me down. I'm going to get back on that Sports desk if it kills me. Mo, I need your help. I've got this high-powered interview at one o'clock tomorrow and nothing but low-octane clothes. Would you go shopping with me tomorrow morning?"

"I'd love it. It'll be just like old times. Do you remember that snowy Saturday when the two of us went to Altman's and bought our first bras?"

"Oh, Lord!" Rainey whooped. "How could I forget? Remember how the clerk was absolutely stony-faced when you said, very grandly, 'Don't bother to wrap them. We'll wear them home'?"

"Then we met my mother for tea at the Plaza, and she was so annoyed with us because we alternated between sticking out our chests and twitching."

"We'd forgotten to take the tags off, and they itched."

Mo sighed. "It seems like a million years ago. Meet me at Barneys tomorrow at ten. You're going to buy yourself a power suit."

Quinn lumbered across the bed with the closet door.

"We were on the evening news," she called after him.

"And we'll be in Billings's story of the affair tomorrow morning." He threw himself across the bed and disconnected the phone. "Let's pretend we're a thousand miles from here, where no one watches the evening news—"

"Or reads newspapers."

He folded her into his arms, saying, "I've thought about you about a million times today. I need you," he murmured, his mouth claiming hers. "Need you . . . need you . . ."

The words, as always, thrilled her, and she melted into him, her body so alive to his touch that pulsating fires racked her limbs.

TOO DAZED, too languid to move, they lay where they had fallen, legs and arms intertwined in a deliciously complicated puzzle, the air prickly on her drying skin.

"Promise me," he said, his lips against her breast, "you won't let working for that crazy section change you. Promise me you won't go all soft and clinging and mimsy on me."

"Mimsy?" If she had any strength left she'd stroke those wonderful hard muscles bunched over his ribs, but she couldn't lift her arm.

"Wishy-washy and vague and relentlessly cute. Don't let them change you, Rainey. Stay just as you are."

Somewhere she found the strength to stroke his leg with her foot. "And what am I?" she teased, lifting his head to outline his lips with her tongue.

"A tigress!" he hissed, pressing her into the bed.

"HOW WAS the City Hall beat?" she asked between bites of egg roll.

"I dodged that dreary bailiwick. I'll trade you two pot stickers for an egg roll."

"I'll give you two wontons for a sparerib. How did you get out of City Hall?"

"You know Billy who does the photo assignments? He and I go back a long, long way—all the way to the Chicago *Trib*. I talked him into putting me on general Metro stuff. I covered a shooting, the opening of some ditsy light store in SoHo, a selection of some of your choicer summer potholes and open hydrants, and a couple of hours at the Brooklyn Botanical Gardens shooting a meat-eating cactus big enough to star on Broadway. Not such a bad day. Now tell me all about Evil Edie and your appointment tomorrow. Are you going to finish that Moo-shoo?"

When the waiter brought their check he presented them each with a glass of pinkish wine. "Compriments of the house," he said with a shy smile.

"For us?" said Rainey. "Please thank the manager for us."

"Why us?" said Quinn.

"Is prum wine—Wan Fu. Prum wine is wine for rovers, and Madam Wu say you must be rovers." He backed away, blushing.

"To lovers and rovers," she said as she touched her glass to Quinn's. "To those who bide and those who roam—over the hills and far away."

"MISS PEABODY will see you at—" Miss Peabody's secretary consulted her book. "One-oh-three, precisely. She's running late today."

"That's okay," said Rainey. She was deliberately twenty minutes early. She wanted to give herself a little time to snoop around.

"Nugget!" squawked an invisible intercom. "Bring your book."

"Yes, Miss Peabody," said Nugget to the intercom. "If you'll excuse me?" she said to Rainey and disappeared through a nearly concealed door.

There was no one else in this waiting room that appeared to be Miss Peabody's private reception area. Rainey made a few quick notes.

Rug: pale blue and cream, mostly cream. Chinese? Nice. Chairs: Chinese-y. Chippendale? (Look this up.) Walls: cream. Prints, four. Little people in bamboo raincoats and bamboo hats struggling up mountain path in rain. (Is there hidden moral here? A message to clients?)

She dropped her notebook in her pocket and sauntered along the deserted corridor behind Miss Nugget's desk. "Hi!" she called out as she pushed open a door marked Staff Only. A dozen word processors blinked emptily, abandoned by the typing pool in favor of lunch. A printer spurted to life, and she knew she was not alone.

"May I help you?" A mass of curly red hair popped up from behind a monitor, followed by wide-set eyes, a friendly smile and several thousand freckles.

Rainey introduced herself.

"I'm Terry Willard," said the typist. "Gosh, that's a beautiful suit. Could I see the back?"

Rainey blushed. She felt like the world's biggest imposter, but she turned in a slow circle.

"I used to sew," said Terry wistfully. "When my twins were babies and I stayed at home. I could copy anything." She squinted at Rainey's suit. "It needs something, something soft. A flower for your buttonhole, that's what you need." She drew a peach-colored tea rose from a bouquet on her desk.

"I don't think I have a buttonhole." Rainey fingered her lapel. "I mean it's there, but it's sewn shut, or something."

"If you'll take off your jacket, I'll open it for you."

"No, please. Really, I—"

"It's no trouble, honestly." She slipped Rainey's jacket from her shoulders and attacked the stitches with the tiniest scissors Rainey had ever seen.

"Those are beautiful roses," said Rainey. They looked like the merest shadows of peach and apricot caught in a haze of baby's breath.

"Aren't they gorgeous. They're from my team." Her eyes crinkled, and her grin was as wide as pride. "I coach a neighborhood league team."

"That's great. How're you doing?"

"We haven't won a game in three years, but we're trying." Terry slid the rose into Rainey's buttonhole, added a snippet of baby's breath and fastened both with a pin.

"Not once in three years?"

"I've got a bunch of really gutsy little kids." She held Rainey's jacket for her.

"Thank you," said Rainey, touching a cool petal. "Where are your kids from? Where do you play?"

"They're all from my neighborhood—the East Village and Lower East side—we've got this marvelous mix of kids from just about every ethnic group you can name. I think we've got the greatest team in the city. We play up in Central Park at six o'clock on Thursdays. Do you like baseball? Would you like to come to a game?"

"I'd love to," said Rainey. "How long have you worked here?"

"Five years. I burned out as a social worker. This job pays better, and coaching my kids keeps my head straight."

"How's Miss Peabody to work for?"

"Tough, usually fair, and maybe just a little bit crazier than the rest of us."

Bingo! Rainey's silent alarm went off. "Crazy how?" she asked cautiously.

"Let's just say her spring's wound a tad too tight. She should try coaching kids—it's cheaper than going to a shrink and a lot more fun."

"I'm told she has a son. Have you met him? Does she ever bring him into the office?"

Terry's sunny smile went out. "They shipped the kid off to boarding school when he turned seven."

"A-har!" cawed Miss Nugget. "There you are, Miss Archer. Whatever are you doing in here? Miss Peabody is ready for you now. If you'll just come this way. . . ."

"Thanks again for the rose," said Rainey hastily.

"Great suit," said Terry with a grin and the thumbs-up sign.

Her interview with Cynthia Peabody lasted precisely nineteen minutes and thirty-seven seconds. In that time she noted:

Office: beige. C.P. also beige. B. knit dress, single strand pearls. Hair, beige, pulled back & held by ornate comb. (Chinese?) Face pale, cheeks flushed, handshake quick & light, hands very cold. Up: 6:00, C.P. and husband Duckie ride exercise bikes. She reads *Wall Street Journal* while peddling. He reads *Times*. Shower. (Together? Afraid to ask. Not likely.) Breakfast: 7:00. Pineapple juice, granola, tea. He reads *Wall St. Jrnl*. She reads *Times*, *Journal*, *Post*, briefs. (Speed reader?) 7:30 Driver takes them to office for day of lawyering. Daily routine unvarying. Exception—personal trainer supervises her workouts in her office Mon, Wed, Fri. Special diets: none. Hair: Mr. Thornby, 7:45 Tuesday mornings. Weekends at their place in the Hamptons. What does she do there? Works.

"And where do you go when you vacation?" Rainey asked.

"Vacation? Why should I take a vacation? I haven't taken a day off since my son was born and that was eight years ago."

"Don't you ever want to take time off to . . . oh, I don't know, to smell the roses along the way?"

"The law, as they say, is a jealous mistress."

"Is that what they say?" asked Rainey.

"There is only one way for a woman to rise to the top of this profession and that is through sheer, unremitting slogging. I slogged my way through college, I slogged my way through law school, and I slogged my way through this firm and into a partnership."

"You must love the law," said Rainey.

"That's too naive for words," she sneered. "This is not for publication, you understand, but it's the power I love, the control. You can't even imagine how exciting it is to mastermind a hostile takeover and succeed. That's worth all the pressure. Shall I tell you what I do when the pressure really builds up?"

"Please," said Rainey.

"Do you really think your readers care about that sort of thing?"

"I'm sure they do," said Rainey. Edie would love this, whatever it was.

"The truth is, I meditate. When the walls start closing in, I kick off my shoes, pull up my skirt, get down on the carpet, and sit cross-legged in the lotus position. I imagine I'm sitting on a cloud. Then I picture the cloud rising and... I know you won't believe this, but after a time I can feel myself rising from the floor."

Hands before her, Rainey held one palm above the other. "You actually rise from the floor." She raised her palm.

Cynthia Peabody nodded, a shy smile softened her face.

"How far do you rise?"

"Two or three inches. Far enough to feel the air beneath me. All my cares float from me then. If I couldn't float I don't know what I'd do. You should try meditating. Believe me, it's better than sex."

Rainey laughed nervously. Cynthia Peabody couldn't be serious. Better than sex? Desperate to change the subject she said, "I understand your husband is with the firm. What is his specialty?"

"Anything he can catch in the typing pool," she snapped bitterly. "Only a fool puts her trust in men, my dear. Put your trust in your work. Your work will never let you down."

"DO YOU REALIZE what tonight is?" said Quinn.

It was after ten, and they had polished off two racks of ribs with 5-Alarm sauce, a thicket of fries and a cubic yard of cole slaw at a new barbecue place on the West Side called Piglet's Revenge. All but bursting, they strolled down to Doyle's. He had an insurance form Rainey had to sign.

"Tonight's the gala," said Quinn. "And the little twerp never even sent us a couple of seats."

"He might have." She was trying to be fair. "It's always possible he sent them to the Sports desk and Wolfe ate them. Let's forget him. If I never hear his name again it'll be too soon."

Quinn slipped his arm around her waist and kissed her hair.

She tucked her hand into his back pocket and pressed her head against his shoulder. Even before they had ever made love there had been an excitement in being next to Quinn that made her tingle all over, as though she'd plugged a finger into a low-voltage socket. But now—now that there was not one square inch of her body he had not kissed, now that she knew the astonishing heights of passion to which he could take her—walking beside him, their bodies touching, was like wading through a molten sea of suppressed passion. He had only to touch her for the throbbing to start again, deep within her.

Part of the excitement was in walking down Broadway and knowing no passerby suspected the stirring within her, while another part of the excitement was knowing that Quinn knew. He always knew exactly how he made her feel, and she knew how much that excited him.

Doyle said, "Quinn, you must be doing something right, I've never seen Rainey look so happy."

"Give me a break, Doyle." She could feel herself flushing clear up to her hair. "Where's that insurance paper you wanted me to sign? I'm really sorry about this."

"Forget it," said Doyle. "Listen, you live in New York, it happens."

She had just finished telling Quinn all about Cynthia Peabody, LADY LAWYER LEVITATES, when she heard a deep Slavic baritone bellow down the bar.

"Comrades!" rumbled Boris.

"Quinn," she said. "He's going to kill us."

"No, he's not," said Quinn. "That's a smile."

She looked again. Indeed, Boris looked like a glossy Moskovite cat who'd swallowed a very sassy canary.

"I come drink your healths with Cloud, that admirable drink Comrade Doyle makes."

It was a dubious Doyle who set a Cloud before Boris. She and Quinn opted for beer.

Boris raised his glass. "Because of you I am now Hero U.S.S.R., Fourth Class."

She looked at Quinn. Quinn looked at her. They both looked at Doyle. All three of them shrugged and turned to Boris.

"Hero?" they sang—a two-note trio.

Boris drew a folded newspaper from his pocket. His eyes shone. "Is first review gala. Just out." He handed her the paper. "Is here at bottom of column. You read."

"Go ahead," said Quinn.

"Read it out loud," said Doyle.

"'A word about Aleksey Kuprin,'" she read from the final paragraph of the review. "'Kuprin, should there be anyone around who still does not know, is the Kirov dancer who defected to the welcoming arms of this company yesterday morning amid hoopla and blaring of trumpets unknown on this island since Mr. P. T. Barnum went to that great big top in the sky. It is inevitable that one casts one's mind back to that glorious evening in July, 1974, when Mikhail Baryshnikov made his debut with another American company, dancing Albrecht to Makarova's Giselle. It would serve no purpose other than grisly curiosity to supply readers with a point-by-point comparison of Kuprin and Baryshnikov. Suffice it to say that Kuprin is a klutz.'"

She looked up to see Boris doubled over in silent laughter. Tears of mirth gushed from his aluminum eyes and plopped into his Cloud.

"A klutz?" she said.

Boris thumped himself on the chest. "Boris Sergey-evitch Tolinkov is hero because he dump dancer on you. Believe me, we don't want him. A dancer like Kuprin nobody is needing."

"Wouldn't you like to see our publisher's wife when she reads this?" said Rainey.

"Marion and Kuprin," said Quinn, "are a match made in heaven."

9

"UPBEAT," said Edie. "Upbeat is the name of the game."

Rainey was trying to get Edie to see some virtue in writing about women more typical than her levitating lawyer had turned out to be. But after reading Rainey's summary Edie was now afraid she might miss a trend.

"I wonder," said Edie, "if transcendental meditation is making a comeback?" She bit her lip and squinted at Rainey. "Do you think it's coming back?"

Rainey shrugged. Edie would have to get her reassurance from someone who cared. "I don't understand who you think our readers are," she said. "Or what their priorities are. Let's be honest. Who really gives a damn about some power-mad lady lawyer with a lousy marriage, a personal exercise trainer and the crazy conviction that she can float four inches above her office floor?"

Edie glowered silently.

"Have you ever ridden the subway and taken a good look at our readers?"

"The subway?" Edie blanched. "You must be joking."

"Our readers are strap-hangers. Our readers don't have personal exercise trainers. Our readers don't worry about corporate assets and bottom lines. They worry about how to pay for their kid's next pair of sneakers."

Edie's bracelets jangled a warning.

Undaunted, Rainey went on. "I met a great subject for a feature story in Peabody's office yesterday. Someone our readers could really identify with."

"Another lawyer?" Hope brightened Edie's eyes.

"A typist."

The light in Edie's glance went out.

"She's a single parent, a woman who cared enough about other people to become a social worker. She cared so much she burned-out. Today she's a typist who coaches a neighborhood league baseball team. Her name's Terry Willard. The kids are—"

"Let me guess. Terry's Pirates? Cute, Archer. Really cute. I think I might throw up. And now you're going to tell me Terry's wunnerful tots are the terror of their league."

"They've never won a game."

"Oh, swell."

"But don't you see," Rainey persisted, "that's my hook. They keep trying."

Edie closed her eyes. "Deliver me," she murmured. Then her eyes popped open and she leaned across the desk. "Upbeat will be the name of the game as long as I'm sitting in this chair. Didn't you learn anything reading our back issues? Life/Style is about winners, Archer. Winners, not losers."

"But you've got it all wrong," said Rainey. "Any kid who loses and goes back knowing he will almost certainly lose again—that kid has learned the real meaning of courage. That's a real winner. Haven't you ever heard what mountain climbers say? You don't conquer the mountain, you conquer yourself. That's what these kids are learning."

Edie sat very still, her bracelets silent. The only sound was the ominous grinding of her molars. "I don't want to hear about this again, Archer. Ever. You are here as a favor to Roland, but I can only put up with so much. Now go finish the Peabody piece."

She put in an hour on the Peabody story but had precious little to show for it. Her heart just wasn't in it. *I'm a reporter,* she tried telling herself, *my heart isn't supposed to be in it.* She watched Maxine instead.

Maxine wrote a weekly column on trendy food. Someone had told Rainey that it was Maxine who had told all New York, months ahead of its actual arrival, that blackened redfish was coming. Conversely, she predicted to the very week, the time when sushi would be out. Maxine's desk backed Rainey's. This morning it was covered with yoghurt containers.

"Got a winner?" asked Rainey just as her phone buzzed.

Maxine licked her spoon and sighed. "You can forget about artichoke, but the apricot chiffon is to die."

"Archer..." she muttered as she automatically tucked the phone between her jaw and her shoulder and grabbed a pencil. "How about a taste?" she said to Maxine.

"Honey," said Quinn in a soft, rumbly baritone that made her tingle all over, "that's just what I had in mind."

"Is it?" she said. "What else is on your mind?"

And for several minutes, while she sat quite still and watched Maxine lick her little white plastic spoons, Quinn told her exactly what he had in mind. She didn't know where to look or what to do. No one had ever said such things to her before, not on a phone. Not at her desk. All around her people were buzzing away at their officey tasks, while she listened to Quinn tell her what he liked best about last night. How was she supposed to get through the rest of the day after listening to him? How could she concentrate on her job?

Maxine peered at her. Could she tell? "Later," she said to Quinn urgently. "I'll see you later."

"You bet you will," he said with a chuckle.

Maxine, who had been observing her covertly for the past several minutes, leaned across the desk the moment she put down the phone. "I'm sure you must have a food allergy." Maxine always brimmed with clinical interest. "What did you have for breakfast?"

"Why?" She could feel perspiration standing in beads on her forehead.

"You're the color of beet borscht, and I'll swear I heard you panting. If you're having problems I've got the most divine allergist...."

"It's nothing really," she mumbled as she dashed for the ladies' and a basin of cold water to splash on her face.

It was Maxine who got her involved with soup. "It's going to be soup," Maxine had said. "I can feel it in my bones." And so she began a series of columns on soups. "It's all cyclical," she explained. "Remember when we were all eating radiccio salads and warm duck breast with—"

"Raspberry vinegar," said Rainey. "Then it was hot and cold noodles. I used to go with a guy who was positively weird about Thai noodles—"

Maxine laughed. "With chopped peanuts and coriander, right?"

"Oh, yeah! And lemon grass? Remember when everything was made with lemon grass?"

"And no one ate, but everyone grazed? It's over," asserted Maxine. "This season it's soup."

Maxine's decree having gone out some months before, it was. No one now was ever heard to mention sushi, not even in passing. Noodles were out. No one brown-bagged it anymore—at least not in the literal sense. Instead, the high-tech thermos had come into its own, for everyone now lunched on soup. Cold soups, hot soups, thin soups, thick soups, vegetable soups, meat soups, fish soups, bird's nest soups.

Maxine flipped through a file and tossed a recipe across to Rainey's desk. "Would you try that for me?" Maxine was notorious for recruiting co-workers, because their food editor refused to allow anyone access to his trial kitchen.

Rainey glanced through the recipe. "Peach soup?" What would Quinn say to peach soup?

"I knew you would," chirped Maxine, before she could answer.

"You won't get anything like this in Borneo," said Rainey.

"What is it?" said Quinn.

"Soup."

"I thought it might be." He stared into the bowl of pale orange sludge.

She had spent an hour on Maxine's peach soup. It tasted like canned fruit salad. "Be honest. What do you think? Tell me the truth. I promised Maxine a report tomorrow morning."

"I always tell the truth." He put down his spoon.

"Well?"

"It tastes like dessert in an orphanage."

"I know, but what am I going to tell Maxine? She really believes in these recipes."

"Tell her it will never replace meat loaf."

"I can't do that."

"Then you'll have to make up something—tell her you couldn't make it because your blender motor burned out. That sounds plausible, doesn't it?" He scraped both servings into the sink and turned on the water. "People will believe anything, if they want to badly enough. Let's go get a couple of cheese-burgers."

While they ate he told her about photographing the jungles in Borneo, how his shirt rotted off his back, and green stuff grew all over his camera bag during the monsoon season.

"Where do you think they'll send you?" she asked. "Have you any idea?" She wished she could put the fact of his leaving out of her mind, but hard as she tried it was always there, like a shadow on a sunny wall.

"Bonn, probably. Or it could be Paris, or Rome. If they sent me to Paris, it would be easy to fly back here to be with you. Or, you could fly over to Paris."

"LONG DISTANCE LOVERS GRAB HOLIDAY?" She shook her head sadly. "I don't know, Quinn. It wouldn't really be the same, would it? I can't believe that sort of thing ever works. Not for long, anyway."

"No," he said ruefully, "I suppose not."

"Let's not talk about it. We promised ourselves we would take each day as a gift. Talking about the future just drains all the sun out."

Later that night she said, "Quinn, are you asleep?"

"Yes," he sighed.

"I'm going to tell her the soup was awful."

"I thought you would," he said.

AFTER EDIE RAN her story on Cynthia Peabody, Rainey brought up her neighborhood league story idea again. Edie raised one perfectly drawn eyebrow, handed her an assignment slip and pointed to the door. Her bracelets jangled. "Upbeat, Archer, upbeat. This Ocean kid's a comer." Rainey looked at the slip. It was an address in SoHo, the area south of Houston Street and east of Little Italy that had become a kind of mother lode of promising artists and craftspeople.

"And phone in when you've finished," said Edie. "I'll have something else for you by then."

Ocean's proved to be a narrow storefront, its walls painted a gentle gray. Projectors concealed in the ceiling threw ever-changing images of water everywhere: calm seas, foam-tossed seas, wind-torn spindrift, brisk waves sinking to placid tidal pools. Piped through quadraphonic speakers came the crash and thud of waves on a pebbled shore, the growl of granite pebbles grinding modulated to the muffled hiss of long slow rollers breaking on a slope of sand, the creak of rigging, the poignant cries of terns and gulls. Velvet-lined cases displayed elaborate necklaces intricately assembled from what appeared to be gold-plated fish bones.

"Miss Ocean?" she called through the gurgling surf.

Miss Ocean flapped out of the back of the shop, as graceless as some soaring seabird forced to get about on shore. She swooped across to Rainey and dipped her head. She had vivid blue eyes, a beaky nose and a small bright mouth. Swept abruptly back from her forehead was a flight of ebony hair—flung back from the temples and blazoned with blond lightning bolts, one above each ear.

"Hi!" said Miss Ocean. "You're with the *Journal*? Well, what do you think?"

Rainey was not sure whether her opinion was being solicited on the jewelry, Miss Ocean's hair, the shop decor or the sound effects. Then it came to her that it was all these things—the total effect. She searched for the right word to fit with the SoHo idiom. "It's *elemental*," she said finally.

"You dig it!"

"Hmm."

"I'll tell you how I started. I read one day where Picasso got like up from his lunch with this perfectly intact skeleton of whatever fish he'd just eaten and like rushed off to his studio and painted it, and I thought: Hey! Y'know?"

Rainey waited, but Miss Ocean merely smiled glassily. "And then?" she prompted finally.

"I said to myself, if it's good enough for old Pablo it's good enough for me. So I plated what was left of a smoked whitefish and started stringing. I knew from the beginning I was on the right track. The sea is like our mother, y'know? We all like crawled out of the primordial ooze, y'know? So I like figured I'd only make things that would help keep people in touch with Mother Sea. Y'know? After I sold my first piece I changed my name to Ocean."

Was there, she wondered, some simple reason for Ocean's infatuation with water and things fishy? It wasn't hard to imagine her as a five-year-old stumping across the sand with a pail in one hand and a leaking starfish in the other. "Did you grow up beside the sea?"

"Don't I wish," sighed Ocean. "Honey, I'm Fayette Bassleiter from Cape Girardeau, Missouri, and that's about as far from the ocean as you can get. But that's not for publication," she added hastily. "Don't print that."

"Why not?" said Rainey. "What's wrong with Cape Girardeau, Missouri?"

"I'm trying to like create an image here, y'know? You gotta be something special to make it in this town, something exotic. I mean who's going to want to buy gold-plated fishbones from somebody from Missouri? Where's the romance?"

"I always thought it was where you found it," said Rainey, too softly for Ocean to hear.

"Next month I'm going to be..." She paused to give Rainey time to brace herself for the full import of what was coming. "...in *Vogue!*" she breathed reverently. "Billy Beau's stylist used my necklaces for a center spread of models at the Fulton Fish Market. *Vanity Fair* was here yesterday, and your paper sent a photographer around this morning. Gorgeous guy. Built like a sailor, y'know? I've got like this thing for sailors. He can dock his dinghy in my harbor anytime."

"I don't suppose you remember his name," said Rainey.

"Winn? Finn? Quinn? Something like that. I really felt like a surge when I talked to him—he was very sensitive to the basic primitive urges the sea stirs in all of us."

"Was he?"

"Oh, yeah. He told me all about paddling a small boat up some river in Borneo."

"Did he really? And was that during the monsoon?"

"I don't remember anything about a monsoon, but he did say he ran out of food and had to live on peaches."

SHE WASN'T AT ALL SURE how it happened. The last thing she remembered clearly was phoning Edie from a deli near Ocean's and Edie sending her to Bloomingdale's to do a story on the new Italian sportswear, which Edie now predicted would soon be taking the country by storm. But all the way uptown she'd been thinking about Quinn, and then as she made her way through the cosmetic department to the escalator she was distracted by a smiling young woman who sprayed her with a new perfume called *Brise de mer*. The scent was so delicious she rode up the escalator sniffing at her wrist and picturing Quinn striding through souks in far-off lands where women's eyes were dark with kohl and the soles of their feet bright with henna. Before she knew what she was doing she got off at the wrong floor, stumbled into a boutique of designer originals and fell desperately in love with a wisp of a dress covered entirely with bugle beads.

Three Raineys twirled in the dressing room mirrors, three Raineys sparkling with electric-blue beads, and she knew she had never wanted anything in the entire world as much as she wanted that dress. *Wait until Quinn sees this,* she said to her smiling reflection. *He'll go wild, absolutely wild. I'll show him something about the basic primitive urges the sea stirs in all of us.*

Am I jealous? she wondered as she waited for a cross-town bus. "You bet your bugle beads," she said to the startled bus driver. *If he's really making passes at that Missouri mermaid, I'll kill him.*

"QUINN? she called out as she opened the apartment door.

A white dust hazed the air. She squinted into the kitchen. It looked like mutiny in a flour mill. PILLSBURY DOUGH-BOY RUNS AMOK. Somewhere behind the clouds of white, Quinn swore. Next came the sound of rending plaster. When the dust settled she saw him, stripped to the waist, his head and shoulders white with plaster, a crowbar dangling from his hand. Her cabinets had disappeared from one wall, the stove had been pulled out, and chunks of plaster lay everywhere. Behind the lath and studs red brick winked darkly.

"What are you doing?" she croaked and then coughed.

"I'm tearing out this wall."

"But you can't do that—"

"The kitchen will look sensational with exposed brick—"

"My landlord will murder me."

"No he won't." He rammed his crowbar behind the lath and levered manfully. A four-foot section of ancient plaster flopped at his feet. He turned to her with a brilliant grin. "Trust me," he said.

"He'll keep my security deposit forever."

Quinn shook his head and plaster dust showered down around him. "This is what's known as improving the lessor's property."

"When my landlord brings suit he's going to call it willful destruction of property. I'll be blackballed. Landlords keep a list, you know. They pass it around to other landlords. I'll never get another apartment in Manhattan as long as I live. You're talking major renovation here. You're talking permits. Electricians. City inspectors—"

Quinn dropped his crowbar on a pile of rubble, starting a white cloud of dust. "Think of the possibilities," he said. "Try to imagine how great this is going to look. Use your imagination, Rainey. Picture that red brick glowing in the morning sun..." He gestured toward the wall as he spoke and at every movement bits of plaster flew from him.

"Oh, Quinn." Her heart flopped over. He wasn't demolishing; in his own funny way he was building.

It fitted right in with painting her walls. *He's nesting*, she told herself. Just like the wild animals he talked about. He was making a nest for himself and his mate. Did a bird make a nest for a mate he planned to leave? Maybe he was staying. Maybe he'd changed his mind and he didn't even know it himself, yet. It could be one of those mysterious, unconscious things. On the other hand, maybe he felt he owed her something. Maybe this was his way of saying thank-you.

The freshly painted walls, she had grown accustomed to, but now whenever she walked into the kitchen and saw that red brick wall, it would be Quinn's kitchen, Quinn's wall. She had friends whose lovers had taken off for parts both known and unknown, and they had left behind sweetly sentimental tokens like fur coats, or gold bracelets, or in one case, a Cuisinart. But a wall? Who ever heard of a lover giving you a wall?

"It's going to be beautiful," he said, wrapping her in his dusty arms. "You'll see. Trust me. Would I lie to you, darling?"

His kisses were salty and gritty, and he smelled of plaster and sweat, and she thought, *If I could bottle this I'd make a fortune.*

"THEY WON'T let us in there," said Quinn. "Look at that crowd on the sidewalk."

Merengue, si! was the in place to dance—this month anyway—and Rainey was determined to go dancing with Quinn. What good was an investment in bugle beads if she didn't cash in on it? She flashed her most ravishing smile and her press pass, and the bouncer on the door made way for them. The music crashed down on them with the insistence of a jet engine.

"Do you see who I see over there?" She pointed to a table beside the dance floor, a table completely surrounded with pale girls of excruciating thinness.

"Poor Kuprin," said Quinn. "He wanted big womans, but it looks like he's stuck with this year's crop of women's underwear models. He's waving. Should I wring his neck?"

"Not until I find out if there's a story here."

"Forget him," said Quinn. "We came to dance. Don't you ever leave your reporter's hat at home?"

"Be fair, darling. What about that time we started out for the movies and ended up spending the whole day in Central Park photographing toadstools?"

"Not toadstools, edible fungi. Mushrooms."

"Just give me five minutes," she said, pulling a reluctant Quinn through the crowd toward the gaily waving Kuprin.

"Come," said the all too familiar voice. "Sit. Have drinks with me. I buy."

"Kuprin," she said. "What are you doing here?"

"I come every night to dance. Bring friends. Girl friends. Come, you and Quinn have drinks. You will cerebrate my new tour?"

"New tour?" she echoed.

"You did not follow my last tour?"

"No," said Quinn.

Kuprin shrugged. "Is okay. Reviews not so hot, anyway. Tomorrow I begin new circuit: Waukegan, Yellow Knife, Moose Jaw . . . these are quaint names, yes? . . . and Casper."

"Are you happy?" she said.

In answer, he dug into his pocket. "Look," he commanded, holding up a gold credit card. "I go nowhere without it."

"Let's dance," said Quinn. "That's what we came for."

Kuprin waved them off, and Quinn pulled her onto the dance floor. His hips swiveled, his back arched, he guided her effortlessly through intricate and surprising patterns. They moved with the blatant beat, their bodies answering each other in a rising frenzy, riding the cresting sound.

"Where did you learn to dance like this?" she panted. She couldn't take her eyes off his hips.

He bent over her. "In the Congo." To make himself heard he spoke with his mouth to her ear, and his hot breath and mischievous tongue sent her into orbit.

"Oh, Quinn," she gasped.

He spun away and then back to her. "Let's get out of here," he said into her ear, "before I tear that dress off you."

"You wouldn't," she shouted, but a wild look in his eye made her dash for the door.

10

A DOZEN gigantic plastic bags were massed at the curb in front of her building. Rainey spotted them from half a block away. They made a tidy green bunker and held the plaster remnants of her kitchen wall. Quinn must have come home from work before her and carried them down. What would she say to Dino, the super?

"Good evening, hey?" said Dino. His gold tooth winked. "You and Mr. Quinn fix up?"

She stared down at him and nodded dumbly, mesmerized as always by the lasciviousness brimming in his doggy-brown eyes.

"You give him this, hey?" He handed her a coil of orange extension cord. "And tell him I don't need the saw before tomorrow."

"Thank you," she said. Saw? What saw? She started up the stairs two at a time.

"You've got it," said Quinn after a long and satisfying kiss in the kitchen doorway. "Now I can take out these last pieces of lath. The cord on the saw isn't long enough."

"You borrowed these things from Dino?"

"He thinks it looks great. I think it looks great. How do you think it looks?"

"Great," she said. "Just great." What else could she say? If the man she adored had set his heart on a brick wall in the kitchen, she wasn't going to tell him it looked like the side of a suburban garage.

Quinn cut away the lath and the wall stood revealed—very red, very rough and garlanded with spider webs sagging with plaster dust.

"It's almost done," he whooped. He picked her up and whirled her in a circle, just as he had done that night at Mo's. "Dust it down, seal it, rehang the cabinets, and it's finished."

"Is that all? Then this calls for a celebration." She ruffled his hair and sawdust sprayed down on his shoulders.

He set her back on her feet, and his hands slid down her back to her thighs. "What did you have in mind, little lady?"

She pressed herself hard against him. "This is Thursday."

He nibbled on her lower lip. "You're very sexy on Thursdays, even in that suit."

"But this is my power suit from Barneys. I thought you liked my suit."

"Compared to that dress with all the little beads, it makes you look like a sex-crazed loan officer." He kissed her again. "What's so special about Thursday?"

"If we grab a fast shower we can catch Terry's kids' game before it's over. I want to try the idea on Edie again tomorrow. But this time I want to have the story roughed out and the pix in hand. Your pix, if you'll do it."

Quinn laughed. "It's going to cost you...." His hands slid back up her thighs.

She bit his chin. "Quick," she said. "Last one in the shower is a—"

But his mouth covered hers and his hands found her breasts, and the last thing she remembered before the fire within her pulled her out of herself and into another world was Quinn murmuring, "One inning now, we'll play the rest of the game later."

TERRY'S PIRATES did not play quite the game she and Quinn expected. They lost by only one run. For the first time in his short history Pinky Estavez, the Pirate's diminutive third baseman, connected with a pitch and socked the ball so far beyond the center fielder's reach that two runs scored. Quinn got at least ten shots of Pinky being carried off the field on his teammates' shoulders amid the cheers of the half-dozen parents who witnessed the astonishing near win. Through it all, Terry, with tears of joy running down her cheeks, jumped up and down on the sidelines and shouted lustily.

Much later that evening, after Rainey and Quinn had picked up their loving game where they'd left off, only to decide, after several more innings, to call it a tie, Rainey said sleepily, "Edie can't turn the story down now. She just can't. It's going to be the best piece I've ever done."

Quinn stretched lazily. "Don't count your chickens."

As GOOD AS HIS WORD, Quinn had his prints of the game sent to her desk by noon. They were marvelous—shot after shot of the happiest, proudest little kids she'd ever seen. Edie couldn't fail to be caught up in such joy, such heart-warming examples of old-fashioned dogged determination and grit.

She was trying to breathe some life into a story on a new lingerie boutique, SILK AND SHIMMIES RETURN, when Maxine threw herself into her chair.

Her face was as pale as paper and her hands shook. "So help me," said Maxine through clenched teeth, "I'm going to kill her."

Rainey didn't have to ask. It had to be Edie. "What happened?" Rainey asked gently.

"She killed my eggplant story. Can you believe it? I spent four days researching this fabulous piece on how everyone is rediscovering eggplant, and she killed it."

"But why? She must have known you were writing it."

"She's decided she hates eggplant."

"But you told me yourself your readers love eggplant."

"That fact and a dollar bill will get you a ride on the subway. She said to tell you she's ready to see you now."

"Oh, boy," said Rainey. "Here we go." She grabbed up her rough draft of TERRY'S PIRATES—WINNERS ALL, added a selection of Quinn's pix and headed for Edie's door. She could hear Edie's bracelets jangling even before she turned the knob.

It didn't take long to lay it all out for Edie. Rainey did not allude to the fact that Edie had turned the story down before. She trusted to her account of the team's history, their inspiring woman coach, and their final near-triumph to carry the day. Quinn's touching and joyful pictures she fanned out across Edie's desk. She tried to keep her emotions out of it, to emphasize the human-interest appeal that would grab their readers.

Edie leaned back, her arms folded across her chest, her bracelets ominously silent.

"There isn't a *Journal* reader out there," Rainey concluded, "who will be able to read this story without a lump in her throat. It's a winner. A real winner. And these pictures of Quinn's…" Her words dropped into the thickening silence and disappeared. She heard a roaring in her ears as though waves were closing over her as she went down for the third time. She fought her way back to the surface in time to hear Edie's bracelets start up again.

"In a word," said Edie. "No. En-oh! I don't see how I can make myself any plainer than that. I don't run stories about losers. And that's it."

"But that's the whole point," she insisted. "They're only losers in a technical sense. In every other sense these kids are winners."

"They lost," sneered Edie.

"If I came up with a loser's diet, you'd love it."

"You bet I would. Diets sell papers. Give me a new diet and you're giving me hope. Hope is upbeat. Hope sells papers. Hopeless kids do not sell papers."

"Is that all you care about, selling papers? What about uplifting the reader, informing the reader? What ever happened to *pro bono publico*?"

"I don't speak Spanish," said Edie haughtily.

"If you run this story," promised Rainey, "you'll get more letters from readers than all your diet features and celebrations of opulence ever brought in."

Edie shuffled her story and pix into their folder and tossed it at Rainey. "Archer, let me tell you something. This is my show. When I say no, I mean no. I do not expect you to argue with me. You have a choice. You can write the stories I assign and write them my way, or you can pick up your check."

Rainey drew herself up to her full five foot ten and stalked to the door. "You can mail it to me."

"What happened in there?" said Maxine, "You look like St. George after he chopped the dragon into pâté."

"I've just quit," she said, still not quite believing it herself. "There comes a time in every woman's life when she has to stick up for her principles, and I just did it."

"Gee," marveled Maxine, "I wish I had your nerve."

It took but a moment to empty out her desk. She turned the drawer upside down on the desk top—it was full of all those fond and foolish notes of Quinn's—and swept the contents into her shoulder bag. The last thing she did was call Billy, who handled the photo assignments, and asked him where he'd sent Quinn. Quinn was back from assignment and in a meeting. She left a message with Billy that Quinn could find her at Doyle's.

Angry, but triumphant, she paced the mercilessly hot streets that were so rank with the burned-rust smell of blasted iron, the sour smell of hopeless people. Lowering, dirty clouds threatened rain. This would be her beat now. She'd never get to cover a ball game if she lived to be 105. Where was she going to find a paper that would hire her to write about anything? There had to be one somewhere. She'd find it. Somehow. Everyone, she decided, should walk out on an Edie at least once in her life.

The air in Doyle's washed over her, so cold and dry she gasped, the perspiration drying on her body made her skin prickle. She peered into the dimness. In the slow watches of the afternoon the place was nearly empty.

"Hey!" said Doyle. "What's up? You look like you've just won the lottery."

"I do?" She looked at her reflection in the mirror behind the back bar. Her cheeks were flushed, her eyes shone, and those lines that had been multiplying in her forehead were smoothed away. It was either relief they both saw in her face, or a high fever.

"So, what happened?"

"Bring me some coffee and I'll tell you all about it."

"Hey!" shouted Quinn from the doorway. "Are you all right?" He sprinted the length of the bar to take her in his arms. "What happened? Everyone's saying you walked out on Evil Edie, that you told her exactly where she could put her—"

"Life/Style section. Quinn, I've written my last story about the Cynthia Peabodys of this world. From now on I'm going to write about nothing but real people."

"Who for?"

"I don't know yet. I have to start looking for a job."

Quinn stared at her as though seeing her for the first time. Was he going to tell her she was crazy? He didn't look like he thought she was crazy, he looked happy and, oddly enough, relieved.

"Then you can come with me," he said. A wide, happy grin split his face. A fond, goofy grin. No one grinned like that anymore, not since Gary Cooper. "This is wonderful! This is fantastic!" He hugged her. "They just told me about it an hour ago, and I've been trying to figure out how to tell you I'm being shipped out, and now I don't have to. We can go together."

"Go where?" she asked, suspicion tightening her throat.

"Nairobi," he said, and after a long pause in which she could hear her blood drumming in her ears, he added, "Kenya. East Africa." And in his voice she heard the same reverence for place she knew her own held when she said Yankee Stadium. He took her hands in his. "I thought they'd give me more warning, give us a chance to prepare . . . I'm covering their election. My plane's at nine tonight."

"That doesn't give us much time, does it? How long will you be gone?"

"Can't say. Could be years. I've been assigned to our Nairobi bureau."

She felt as though she had been saying goodbye to him ever since they met. Yet, she had never expected his going to be quite like this. Or so soon. She needed time to prepare, to steel herself. A wave of nausea washed over her. Sweat trickled down her back. Quinn was leaving. There was nothing she could have done to prepare for this. Quinn was leaving.

He squeezed her hands excitedly. "Come with me. You'll love it over there. While I'm working, you can travel to the game reserves and watch for elephants and lions and wildebeasts."

"Oh, Quinn," she blinked very fast because her eyes stung so. "Be sensible, try to be realistic. Can you really see me, *me*, following animals around a game reserve? I'm a city person, I'm a sportswriter. The furriest thing I've ever written about was a hockey goalie from Montreal. And I'm not even qualified to be someone's cricket and soccer correspondent. I haven't worked all these years to get where I am only to throw it all over and run off to Africa."

"But you're not throwing anything over, you're out of a job."

"I'll find another. There are other papers in this town, other sports editors besides Wolfe."

Quinn grabbed her shoulders and said, "You're marvelous when you're defiant." He kissed her quickly and called to Doyle. "Do you have any champagne?"

"Not that you'd want to drink," said Doyle. "How about a tap beer?"

"Then it'll have to be beer. I want to propose a toast," he said to her. That loopy smile curved his mouth again.

"I won't drink to your leaving," she insisted. "That's a rotten toast." She couldn't kid herself. Life without Quinn was going to be pure, unmitigated hell on wheels.

His eyes twinkled at her. "We'll drink to my staying." He raised his glass, winked and drained it.

"I don't understand," she said.

"Mike Parker over at *International Geographic* offered me an editor's job last week, but I turned him down. I didn't think anything could change my mind about going overseas... until now. Now that I've looked at the cold reality of life over there without you, I can't do it. I'm not going to leave you, Rainey. You're the only reason I've ever come across to stay in one place."

"Wait a minute, Quinn. Not so fast. I can't keep this all straight. You can't give up your foreign assignment for me. I won't let you. It's not right. You'll end up hating me. You can only do it for yourself. And what about making all that extra money for your alimony payments. What about your ex-wife? What about the call of the wild?"

"I don't have an ex-wife."

"What do you mean, you don't have an ex-wife?"

"There's no easy way to tell you this. I've been trying to figure out a way to do it ever since that weekend at Mo's. Champ, I kind of fudged that a little."

"You mean you made it all up."

"Yes."

"All of it?"

"Yes."

"There's no Ilga running a cooking school in Chicago?"

"No."

"I trusted you," she said when she was finally able to speak. "I trusted you." Her voice was harsh, jagged. He tried to catch her hands, but she pushed him away.

"Rainey, I only told you those stories because I knew I'd never get to first base with you if I couldn't find some chink in your armor."

"Armor? What armor?"

"You all but clanked with mistrust that day we met."

"Turns out I was right. Quinn, you're nothing but a wolf in wolf's clothing. Men! You're just like all the rest. There's not a one of you who can be trusted."

"Trust?" he spat angrily. "What do you know about trust? You stopped trusting men when your father died. You can't go on forever blaming all the rest of us because he deserted you by dying when you were still a kid. C'mon, grow up."

"Thanks for the pop psychology. You could do a column for Evil Edie with dumb ideas like that. You don't have a clue to what it's been like to be Ace Archer's daughter."

"Cushy, I should think," he sneered.

Rage rose up in her, a swirling, red-hot anger. Her hands shook. "Not so cushy when it's clear to you even as a little kid that your father wishes you were a son so he could make you into another pitcher. Not so cushy when your father gets killed on an LA free-way driving back from a night with a nubile starlet not much older than you are. Not so cushy when, for your mother's sake, you never admit Ace Archer was anything but the saintly superhero all the fans wanted him to be . . ."

"I'm sorry, Rainey. I'm really sorry."

Whether about Ace's lies or his own she wasn't sure, and she didn't care. "I trusted you, Quinn. Against my better judgment and all my instincts, I trusted you." She could feel hot tears spilling down her cheeks now, but it didn't matter. Let it all hang out, she thought bitterly. What's to lose? "I really thought you were special, Quinn. Deceit was the last thing I expected from you. This world is so full of lies and deceit, so full of phony stories and cheap, plastic people. But you . . . to me you were the last authentic man, a man of honesty and of grace."

"But Champ—"

"Don't Champ me. I don't care whether you go to Kenya, the *Geographic*, or to hell. Just get your stuff together and get out of my apartment and my life." Tears splashed on her hands.

He spun on his heel and strode away, his back ramrod straight, his hands jammed in his pockets. Halfway to the door he turned as if to say something, but instead brushed the air in front of his face with both hands as though shooing away a swarm of gnats. Then he was gone.

Doyle leaned across the bar and thumbed the tears from her cheeks. "Rainey, honey." His voice was gentle, but chiding. "You had no call to tell him those things about Ace. No call at all."

"I've been covering up for Ace since I was fourteen. I'm sick of lying about him."

Doyle rubbed his chin. "It's okay for you, but not for Quinn?"

"Shut up, Doyle. You don't understand, you don't understand at all." And she left him there, polishing the bar in slow lazy circles.

She couldn't go home. She had to give Quinn a chance to clear out. When did he say his plane was? Nine? It was nearly five now. She walked down Eighth to Twenty-third and over to Madison Square. She turned north and headed back uptown. Mechanically, she moved her legs, robotlike she put one foot ahead of the other, and with every step she felt more and more betrayed.

Finally, she walked into Central Park. She had to do something to work off her anger, get it out of her system. Maybe she would rent a rowboat and row around the lake until she was tired enough to go home and sleep. Raindrops splattered on the dusty walk, dark worthless coins. Suddenly she was pulled backward, an arm snaked around her throat, her breathing cruelly cut off. A knee jabbed in the small of her back, a hand tore at her shoulder bag.

"Don't fuss, lady, and you won't get hurt." It was a young voice, but old in guile.

She snapped forward from the hips, jerking her attacker off balance. Quickly she bent double, pulling him onto her back. His grip on her throat tightened as he fought to keep his feet on the ground, but she grabbed his wrist.

"Hey!" he shouted. "Leggo! Leggo my arm, man."

Pulling with all her strength she threw him up and over her back, letting his own weight carry him through an arc that ended with a gratifying thump on the ground.

"My arm!" he screamed. "You near bust my arm."

"Get up, you rotten little creep. Stand up and fight like a man." She poked him with her toe.

He scuttled away, staying close to the ground. "You ain't no cop," he said, rubbing his shoulder. "You too good-lookin' to be fuzz." He scrambled to his feet and fled through the rain toward Fifth Avenue.

It was pouring now. She was soaked to the skin, but she didn't care—she was too amazed at how much better she felt. Maybe she should go back to karate class. It might fill her time now that that lying Quinn was gone. She jogged out of the park, splashing all the way home.

The apartment was so empty it echoed. She looked at the yellow walls and remembered how she had walked in to discover him painting. Unable to face the bedroom, she wandered into the kitchen where the unfinished brick wall smiled at her dustily.

"Shut up!" she said to the wall and grabbed a towel to dry her hair.

Quinn's keys glinted on the kitchen table. Had she made the greatest mistake of her life? Should she have gone with him, forgiven his lies? His keys winked in the half light. He had never pretended to be the marrying kind, or even the sort to stay around. Was this, she wondered, a part of what had appealed to her? Was Quinn her brass ring, and she a damned fool for not grabbing him and hanging on for dear life?

The apartment bell jangled, startling her. Quinn. It had to be Quinn. His keys were in her hand. He couldn't get in without ringing. "I'm coming," she shouted as she raced to the door. "I'm coming!" She fumbled with the locks. "Wait, Quinn. I love you!" She threw open the door and flung herself against an astonished Wolfe.

"You're all wet," said Wolfe. He held her fastidiously at arm's length. "What the hell happened?"

"What are you doing here?"

"That witch from Life/Style has been screaming at me like a maniac for sending you to her section. What's this story you wanted to write and she refused? Aren't you going to ask me in?"

"I've got to get a cab to Kennedy." She slung her bag over her shoulder and pushed him out the door. "I have to catch Quinn before he takes off for Kenya." She clattered down the stairs, swinging wide on the newel post at each landing. Wolfe thudded behind her. She was not going to lose Quinn. She loved him. That was more important than anything.

Rain lashed the dark street and drummed on the parked cars, hail bounced and skidded on the sidewalks.

Wolfe whistled through his teeth. "You'll never get a cab in this downpour. I'll drive you."

"You will?" she said gratefully.

"C'mon, it's on my way." He stepped around a fireplug to unlock a battered sedan. The airport was nowhere near Larchmont, but she wasn't going to press her luck.

"How much time have we got?" said Wolfe as he headed across town.

"Nearly an hour. His flight's at nine o'clock. We can make it easily if you take the tunnel."

"I'm taking the Fifty-ninth Street Bridge."

"But we're going to Kennedy, not LaGuardia. The tunnel's faster for Kennedy. It puts us right on the Long Island Expressway." Why was she telling him all this. Wolfe must know all the routes blindfolded, he'd lived here all his life.

He gripped the steering wheel so hard she thought he might snap it in two. "I don't drive tunnels." He spoke so softly she barely heard him over the drumming rain.

My Lord, she thought. The big bad Wolfe is claustrophobic.

"Give me the straight scoop," he said. "What happened between you and Edie?"

She told him all about Terry and her Pirates. Her ideas for developing the story lasted until they turned onto the bridge and pulled up behind a florist's truck.

"It sounds great," he said. "Write it."

"For whom? I just quit, remember. Besides, I'm going to Kenya." She hadn't realized it until she'd said it. The truck wasn't moving. The lanes on either side weren't moving. Nothing was moving.

He swiveled in his seat. "Whaddaya mean, who for? For me. You're going to write that story for me. I want you back on the Sports desk. And what's all this garbage about going to Kenya?"

"Now that I'm ready to go to Kenya you want me for the Sports desk? It's gridlock, Wolfe. We're trapped in absolute gridlock." They'd never make the plane now.

Lightning crackled overhead. The windshield wipers struggled on, out of sync. *Hurry-up! Hurry-up!* said the left one. *Too-late! Too-late!* answered the right.

Wolfe said, "What are you doing chasing after this guy? You're too good for him."

"No, I'm not. He's a great guy, you just don't know him." Did she know him? How much did she really know? Only that he was a marvelous lover, that she adored him, that she couldn't imagine how she was ever going to live without him, and that he lied like a trooper.

"C'mon, Archer, whaddaya say?"

"Why, Wolfe? Why are you doing this?"

"I need you. You've got a special touch 'cause the guys open up to you in a way they won't open up to Billings, or Cuddy, or any of the other guys. You write well, you're gutsy, you've got a great nose for a story... And I'll be grateful to you for the rest of my life for getting that Edie woman off my back. She's sworn she'll never speak to me again. I can only hope she means it." He rubbed a hand over his face. "Aaah, don't make me go through all this, just say you'll come back. Listen, Lefty Ramirez is retiring from the Yankees. Did you know that? I got the call this morning. He claims he learned his style from watching your father."

"I know." Who taught Quinn his style, she wondered. She was probably nothing more to him than another notch on his gun stock, or his saddle horn, or whatever it was roving cowboys notched. Quinn the rover. She was making a damn fool of herself running after him like this. Her eyes stung furiously. I will not cry, she told herself. I will not humiliate myself in front of Wolfe.

"If you'll interview Ramirez for me, you can cover a Yankees road trip."

She swallowed hard and dug her nails into her palms.

"C'mon, Archer. Whaddaya say?"

"Yes. I say yes, Wolfe. If I can write about Terry and cover the Yankees, I'll come back."

They were moving again. When they reached the other side of the bridge she said, "Turn off here and turn around."

"You don't want to go to Kennedy?"

"It's too late. Much too late."

11

RAINEY STARED at the keys in her hand. She did not want to open her door. Fatigue, utter bone-chilling exhaustion was the only thing keeping her from bolting down the stairs and spending the night in a hotel. Blindly she stabbed at the first lock, then the next. Reluctantly she slipped inside and leaned against the door.

Nothing had physically changed. No chair was overturned, no drawer hung open, hastily abandoned. But every footfall echoed hollowly, her breathing seemed unnaturally loud. The air conditioner wheezed in a sinister new voice. Every vestige of Quinn was gone. No cameras littered the coffee table; the hangers in the front closet clanged emptily when she opened the door. He had even wheeled her bicycle back into the closet and hung up the jacket she'd tossed over the handlebars. Everything was just as it had been before he'd walked into her life, except that nothing would ever be the same now that he'd walked out of her life. The unimportant things were all in their places—it was her heart she knew she could never reassemble. Hearts didn't go back together just like that, she thought. And she never was any good at all that insert-tab-A-in-slot-B stuff. She told herself she was glad he hadn't left a soppy note; that really would have been too much.

She kicked off her shoes and walked across the bed to claim her robe from the closet. There was no way in the world she was going to sleep in that bed. She'd sooner stretch out on a bed of nails. She would have to get rid of it. But how? She ought to be able to find a simple solution to the problem. After all, she had prided herself on being totally self-reliant before she met Quinn. There should be nothing to it, she reasoned. What could be easier than getting a king-size, wall-to-wall bed out of a fifth-floor bedroom? She would talk to Dino, the building super, tomorrow. Dino was a reasonable man who could always be counted on to come to her assistance, if she accompanied her request with a smile, fifty dollars and two passes to Yankee Stadium.

She kicked at the sheet and rolled onto her stomach. How could the sofa be so lumpy? Had Quinn done something to it? *I'm really my mother's daughter*, she thought. *We both have a talent for falling for dangerous men.* She wondered why, whether it might be something encoded in their genes. Life would be so much easier if she could only care about nice, safe men. Guys like Billings and Jellicoe were probably great husbands—so easy, so predictable, so dull. She curled on her side. Would Billings pretend to be broke and sleep on this miserable sofa in order to get into bed with a woman he fancied? Would Jellicoe invent an ex-wife to win her sympathy? Would either of them have put his job on the line to help her in that ill-fated Kuprin affair? Never! She plumped up her pillow and squirmed down on her back. Would Jellicoe call his wife and màke love to her over the phone? Would Billings make love under a plum tree? Too dull, dull, dull. She drifted off into a daze of aching memory—she and Quinn in Mo's garden, watching the morning sun wash the sky.

The ringing telephone frayed the edges of her dream. Groggy, more than half sleep, she wrapped the sheet around her and stumbled after the sound. Now that Quinn had put the phone on a fifty-foot cord, she could never find it. She tracked it to the farthest corner of the bed, threw herself full length across the blanket and grabbed for the receiver.

"I'm sorry to wake you." It was Quinn. He sounded cool, distant and not in the least sorry.

"You!" was, unfortunately, the best she could manage. Heaven help me, she thought, I sound like a made-for-television movie. He couldn't be in Kenya. Even she knew it took hours and hours to get to East Africa. Maybe even days. She didn't care where he was. Perhaps he had never left. Maybe he was still someplace in New York. "So where are you?" she asked casually.

"Amsterdam," said Quinn.

"Oh." She wrapped her arm around his pillow and hugged it close. It smelled of Quinn, and her shampoo and his after-shave. A terrible pain creased her middle. "What are you doing in Amsterdam? I thought you were going to Kenya?"

"First leg of the trip." His voice was as warm and caring as a talking weight machine.

"I accidently left my corduroy jacket in your front closet."

Extra emphasis on the *your*, she noted. And exactly what did he mean by accidently? The place looked like he'd taken everything including his dust with him. Hadn't Freud, or somebody, said there are no accidents?

"I would appreciate it," he continued, "if you'd send it to me in care of the Nairobi bureau."

"I'm sure you're wrong," she said. "I didn't see it."

"You weren't looking for it," he said. "Actually looking."

"Okay, I'll look for it."

"And you'll send it?"

"If it's there, I'll send it."

"It's there," he insisted.

"I said I'd look, didn't I?"

"Thank you," he said with such icy politeness her breath caught in her throat. By the time she had readied her reply he had hung up.

She stared at her watch. It was five o'clock. How was she going to get through the hours until she could reasonably appear at work? And once she'd put in her day at the paper, how would she get through the night? "No!" she said to the ceiling. "I'm not going to punish myself like this. I'm right and Quinn is wrong. And he knows it." She threw Quinn's pillow across the room and out into the hall. Then she buried her face in her own and thought about betrayal.

Had she loved him? She must have. Why would she feel so awful now if she hadn't loved him? Did she love him now? No. No way. The game was over. That's what it had been to Quinn, a game. But it hadn't felt like a game. Quinn had blown into her life as quickly and blindingly as a dust storm on some far Sahara. Now that he was gone the air was supposed to clear. She fell asleep and dreamed she was walking across a desert in which she left no footprints, calling for Quinn in a voice that made no sound.

It was only when she tripped over Quinn's pillow on her way back from the shower that she remembered his corduroy jacket. It was there, she discovered, beneath her raincoat. She shut the door quickly. Once she had dressed, she leaned against the kitchen sink, her cabinets still at her feet, and ate her breakfast orange. The unfinished brick wall stared back at her rosy with reproach. Well, she wasn't going to come home every night and get up every morning to a wall in which every brick reminded her of Quinn. A plasterer could be hired to cover it up. A painter would paint it for her. A carpenter would rehang her cabinets. Yes! She would put her life back together by starting with the wall.

She stopped at the closet to pick up Quinn's jacket. Like his pillow it smelled of Quinn. The corduroy was luxuriously soft, fashionably worn and the color of wheat. She slipped it on and stepped back to examine the effect in the mirror. She turned up the collar and set the lapels. Bloomingdale's would love the shoulders—they were so improbably wide. The sleeves, which flapped down over the ends of her fingers, she pushed up to her elbows. With her sky-blue linen slacks and butter-yellow shirt she needed only a yellow rose in her buttonhole to look like a million bucks. When she sucked in her cheeks and let her eyelids droop she was one of those tough, tender, but always classy dames in the great Hollywood movies of the forties. She was the heroine with too much pride to let any man know how much she needed him. She slung her bag over her shoulder, stuck one hand in her pants pocket and turned back for a final sidelong glance at those fabulous shoulders. "Joan Crawford," she said, "eat your heart out."

As though in consolation, the Sports department was friendlier than it had ever been before. Billings and Cuddy welcomed her back with terrible old jokes, and Jellicoe, as always, tried to get her to split her cheese Danish with him. She spread out her notes on Terry's kids and began working on her story, all the while troubled by an indefinable sense of unease.

Everything was somehow diminished. The room seemed smaller, the air thinner, the surroundings grubbier, her colleagues grayer. Her whole day was like a light bulb dimmed by a power shortage.

Wolfe ran KIDS' LEAGUE LOSERS ARE WINNERS over her byline, and it was such a popular story it brought in a sack of mail. When she interviewed the retiring Ramirez, a skinny kid from Photo took the pix. Her heart just wasn't in it—she seemed to be running on autopilot, though Wolfe's praise was fulsome. He finally sent her to Yankee Stadium where she spent what should have been a faultless afternoon in the press box making notes on the new Yankee pitcher who was supposed to lift them out of their current slump, but, for this day at least, all the savor had leaked away. Amid forty other sportswriters, she stared off into the cobalt sky and tried to tell herself it didn't matter. Doing her job should be enough. But it wasn't enough. She had what she'd always wanted, she had realized her dream, but without Quinn to share it with her, it was as empty and cold as the sky. Covering the Yankees was like a consolation prize.

MR. CARDUCCI HAD TAKEN OVER her kitchen. He had clasped her hand in his callused paw and sworn by St. Joseph that the job would be finished in three days, but after five days he was far from done. To replace the studs Quinn had removed, he nailed strips of wood to the brick wall, and he nailed slowly. To these, he explained, he would fasten plasterboard to give her "a nice, smooth-type wall. Easy clean." He came each morning at eight o'clock and worked until noon when he went off to his regular job, the nature of which she never learned. Mr. Carducci was so old and bent she rushed to help him when she heard him wheezing up the steps, struggling with unwieldy sheets of wallboard.

While Mr. Carducci pounded slowly, she ate an orange in the living room and wondered if the rain would stop in time for this afternoon's game. When the phone rang she traced it to the floor behind the television.

"Hello," said Quinn, and her heart flopped over and quivered like a trout.

"Oh." Her face went hot, her hands cold, and she couldn't breathe. She was furious with herself that she had so little control. *But I want him!* shouted a voice inside her head. *I want him, and I'm going to have him!*

"I wondered if you sent my jacket. It hasn't come."

"Really?"

Whoomp! went Mr. Carducci's hammer. *Whoomp! Whoomp!*

"What's that noise?" said Quinn. "It sounds like someone's hammering."

"He is."

"He who?"

"Vito," she said. "He's replacing the lath on the wall—"

"On *my* wall? How can you let some stranger mess around with my wall?"

"But he's not a stranger. You remember Ellie and Paul talking about Vito, that gorgeous Sicilian who did all their plaster work when they bought the house in Brooklyn Heights. The one Ellie said looked like a Greek statue sugared with plaster dust. Vito, not the house."

"Your friend Ellie's exact words, as I remember them, were that he looked good enough to eat."

"Hmmm." She popped an orange segment into her mouth, chewed and waited.

Finally Quinn said, "I can't figure out what happened to my jacket. I've talked to the postal authorities here twice. I'm sure they think I'm a little bit nuts, but you know how attached I am to that jacket." When she didn't say anything, he added, "You did send it, didn't you?"

"Why wouldn't I?" she asked innocently and wound the phone cord around her finger.

"Women do some pretty weird things when they're angry."

"Do they? Have you ever stopped to ask yourself why? You must have collected enough examples over the years, Quinn. Why don't you write an article about it for Life/Style. That's just the sort of piece Evil

Edie would adore. REVENGE. HOW FAR WILL WOMEN GO?

"You're still angry." His voice was flat, matter-of-fact.

"No, Quinn. I'm not angry. To be angry you have to care. And I've stopped caring." Did he believe her? She knew she'd sound more convincing if her voice didn't quiver so.

"Hey, missus," shouted Mr. Carducci. "You come help me lift?"

"Vito's calling me," she said. "Gotta run."

She stared at the brick wall, it's furring strips now complete, and saw that when the wall was finished there would be a hollow chamber between the strips. "Mr. Carducci," she began. "Could you drive a nail into the brick, say there—?" She pointed to a spot right in the center. "If you stuck a nail there, between these two strips, and I hung something on the nail, your wallboard would fit right over it, wouldn't it? I mean there's plenty of room, isn't there."

Mr. Carducci gave her a look that said at his age there were no surprises left. With one finger he pushed up his ancient fedora. A red line creased his forehead. "Yeah, sure, missus." He dug a nail from his pocket and whacked it into a brick.

She snatched Quinn's jacket from the front closet and thrust it on the nail. "Wall it up," she said grandly. "I never want to see it again."

He rubbed his red forehead. "You sure, missus?"

"Positive!" She turned on her heel and left for work.

BY THE TIME Quinn called again the wall was finished. It was as smooth as rink ice and dazzling in its whiteness. Mr. Cioffi was ready to start painting it for her. Enzo Cioffi was married to Mr. Carducci's sister, Rosa. Not a minute younger than Mr. Carducci, he had refused the job when she confessed there was no elevator, which was why she was lugging his last bucket of paint up the stairs when Quinn called.

"She come," she heard Mr. Cioffi say as she gained the landing. "You wait," he added as she came through the door. He handed her the receiver. "Crazy guy." He pointed to his forehead and waggled his finger in a circle. "Says he's in Africa."

"Who was that?" said Quinn, his voice gratifyingly thick with suspicion.

She smiled at Mr. Cioffi's retreating back. "The man who's going to put some color in my life." She tried to make her voice soft and husky. "His name is . . . Enzo."

"Enzo? Enzo? Are you seeing that Japanese designer you wrote about for Evil Edie?"

"That's Kenzo. Don't you know anything, Quinn? Enzo is a hot-blooded Sicilian."

"What happened to the last hot-blooded Sicilian? Your plasterer?"

"He did everything he knew how to do, Quinn. By the time he left he was an old man."

Quinn groaned. "And what is Enzo doing there at eight in the morning, or shouldn't I ask?"

"Painting, actually. He's going to paint the kitchen. Ellie tells me he has an incredible stroke with a brush."

"I'll kill him!" seethed Quinn.

"Why?" she said. "It's my wall." When he didn't answer, she said, "I suppose you called to tell me your jacket is still missing."

"Why else would I call?" he said casually.

"I'm sure I can't imagine," she answered just as off-handedly.

"Yeah . . . well . . ." he said. They both fell silent. Finally, Quinn cleared his throat. "I saw your piece on Terry's kids."

"You did?"

"This bureau is not exactly the back of beyond, you know. We do have the early edition flown in each day. It was every bit as good as I knew it would be."

"Thank you. That's very gracious of you, really. Your pictures looked terrific."

"Thanks. You didn't tell me you'd gone back to work for Wolfe."

"You didn't ask."

"It was one helluva surprise to turn to the sports page and see your byline. I could hardly believe it."

"Believe it."

"Well, how does it feel to be back?"

"It's all right."

"Just all right? I would have thought you'd be walking on air."

"I did a story yesterday on a pitcher who had a little trouble getting up for the game. At the moment, Quinn, I'm having a little trouble getting up for my life."

"Ouch! Dammit!"

She heard the sharp sound of a slap. "What's wrong?"

"Mosquitoes. I'm calling from a petrol station on the road from Mombasa. The mosquitoes are as big as Wolfe and twice as nasty."

"Do you have your malaria pills? It wouldn't do to forget to take them." She tried to sound coolly practical. Dear God, she prayed silently, don't let him get malaria. Preserve him from mosquitoes and snakes and lions and tigers and charging rhinoceroses. And spiders. Especially spiders.

"Of course I have them. Only a fool would come to Africa without them."

"Well, that's good, then."

"Yes. I'll . . . uh, let you know when the jacket turns up."

"You do that," she said.

"It's bound to show up any day now."

"Hmmm."

"Goodbye," he said. Then he asked, "Is Enzo painting my wall?"

"Goodbye, Quinn," she said and hung up.

That night she lay for hours staring at the ceiling, trying to blink away the headlines that formed and reformed in the darkness. JOURNAL PHOTOGRAPHER MAULED BY LION. JOURNAL PHOTOGRAPHER GORED BY RHINO. JOURNAL PHOTOGRAPHER EATEN BY ARMY ANTS. She sat bolt upright, shivering. She'd forgotten all about the ants.

She'd never sleep now. She got up to make herself a cup of Red Zinger. She sat in her newly painted kitchen, sipped her tea, and wondered what time it was in Nairobi. She found the phone behind the bathroom door and carried it to the kitchen. An assistant night editor on the Foreign desk gave her the number of their Nairobi bureau. With the phone book open at her elbow for easy reference she began to dial, telling herself all the while, this is never going to work. International access was 011, then 254 for Kenya, then 2 for Nairobi. Is that really all there is to it? Last the bureau's local number which looked fatally deficient with its five digits. It was ringing. An efficient secretary told her Mr. Quinn had flown to Isiolo to photograph lions in the Samburu Game Reserve.

With her tea in one hand and the phone in the other, she went back to bed. To their bed. The bed the super said he wouldn't carry downstairs not even if she paid him a million bucks because his back was killing him. It was three in the morning and she had to talk to someone. She dialed Mo and got her answering machine. Well, she wasn't so far gone she was going to hold a conversation with an answering machine. She banged the receiver down, and in the same instant the phone rang, and she jumped straight up in the air and spilled her tea.

"Did I wake you?" asked Quinn hopefully.

"No," she answered testily. "But now I'll have to sleep on the wet spot."

"On *what?*" His voice shook with outrage.

She let him simmer for a four-beat pause before she said, "Tea, Quinn. You made me spill my tea. I'm drinking Zinger. Now I'm going to have a red stain right here in the middle."

"Which sheets are you sleeping on?"

"Why?"

"I'm trying to picture you . . . stretched out in our bed . . ."

"The blue ones, I'm sleeping on the blue ones with the red pinstripe."

"Uh-huh."

"Where are you calling from?" she said.

"A petrol station beside the Isiolo airstrip." He sounded so far away. On the other side of the door to Nothing and Nowhere. "I have a few minutes before my van leaves. I thought I'd give you a call. The jacket's still not turned up, by the way. Did your gaggle of lusty Sicilians finish the kitchen?"

"It's terrific. It looks like something Edie would run in her Thursday home pages. FAST TRACK KITCHENS. Everything's practically iridescent with fresh enamel.

You remember how dark it was with that whole wall of red brick—sort of grungy-cozy. Not any more, let me tell you. Now it's like walking into a hall of mirrors, or an operating theater. It's so bright it's dazzling. I mean you could go snow blind just boiling an egg. It's so cold, so sterile, so forbidding. It's so new. Oh, Quinn, I can't tell you how much I hate it."

There was no sound on the line, only a distant crackling of static.

"I need you, Quinn," she whispered softly to herself. "Why aren't you here?"

She heard a bang, as though the door to Nowhere had slammed shut, then a rush of wind and Quinn's voice burst through a blizzard of static. "What did you say?" he shouted.

"I said, I need you. I need you, you big jerk."

"I love you, too," shouted Quinn. "Can you hear me? I said I love you!" And then the line went dead.

12

"ARCHER!" bellowed Wolfe. "Haven't you finished that piece yet?"

"Almost!" she shouted back. It wasn't the story that was slowing her up, it was the corrections that were giving her such trouble. It was three days since Quinn's last call, and for three days her typing had gone haywire. With each day that passed she found it more and more difficult to concentrate on the work at hand. This afternoon she was trying to write about a pitching coach named Svenquist, but for the first six paragraphs she had called him Quinnquist. Unnerved, she poured herself another cup of coffee, put the story on hold and punched up a fresh screen.

FACT 1: QUINN SAYS HE LOVES ME, she typed at the top.

FACT 2: DO I LOVE Q? YES! HEAVEN HELP ME, I DO.

FACT 3: Q IS UMPTEEN THOUSAND MILES AWAY.

FACT 4: I'M HERE.

FACT 5: 1+2+3+4=GOOSE EGG. ZERO. ZIP!

CONCLUSION: WHO EVER SAID 'DISTANCE LENDS ENCHANTMENT' WAS OUT OF HIS COTTON-PICKIN' MIND. IT HURTS LIKE HELL.

She erased the screen and called up her story, taking particular pains not to type Quinnquist, but Svenquist. When she finished the final paragraph, she reread the story from the top. This time she had made a worse hash of it. She had typed Svenquinn, inserted Nairobi for Nyack and Mombasa for Minneapolis.

"Archer!" bellowed Wolfe. "You'll miss your plane."

"I'm finished, I'm finished!" Grimly she made her corrections, sent the story to memory and ordered a hard copy for Wolfe to go over.

"No, you're not," said Quinn.

"Quinn!" She couldn't believe it. Could she be hallucinating? She spun out of her chair with a leap Kuprin would have envied and landed in Quinn's arms. He was as solid and real as she could ever want. "What are you doing here? How come you're back? How long can you stay?" she asked between breathless kisses.

Cuddy whistled. Jellicoe applauded, and Billings made rude noises.

"Let's get out of here," said Quinn. "Let's go home. I need a shower and some sleep, I haven't slept for days." He looked thinner, felt bonier. His face and hands were burned to a deep mahogany and there were circles under his eyes. "We've got a lot to talk about."

"WANDERING PHOTOG RETURNS," called Wolfe as he hurried toward them. "Hey!" He punched Quinn on the arm. "That's a great tan, fella. Good to see you again. Archer can't go anywhere with you, she has to grab the Boston shuttle in time to cover the Yankees-Sox game tonight."

Quinn stared at Wolfe, his eyes wide with disbelief. "You're sending Rainey to cover the Yankees?"

"You're damn right. She's good. Don't you know that? Don't you ever read her stuff?"

Quinn blinked. "I've always known that. But I came back to get married, to have a honeymoon, and—"

"Quinn," she said, "do you mean that?"

"Of course I mean it. You can't call it a proper marriage without a honeymoon."

"I mean about getting married."

"Don't you want to marry me? Are you still sore? I thought you loved me."

"I do love you. You know I love you. And I know you love me. But what does that get us? Married won't matter, it won't change anything. You'll be a married man in Nairobi, and I'll be your wife back in New York."

"No, that's where you've got it wrong. I'm going to be your husband in New York."

"Really, Quinn? Do you really mean that?"

"What's a guy to do when he can't get a decent cheeseburger in all of Africa?" Grinning, he kissed her, and said, "Let's go down to City Hall right now."

"Now, hang on there," said Wolfe. "Can't it wait a couple of hours? You can get married in Boston. Boston oughtta be a great place to get married. Very historic, Boston. You could even tie the knot in the press box at Fenway Park. Before the game. After the game. Maybe work it into the seventh inning stretch. Whaddaya say? Rainey covers the road trip, you take the pix."

"But I've quit the *Journal*," Quinn protested. "I'm going to work as an editor for the *International Geographic*."

"Darling!" she began, but Wolfe interrupted.

"C'mon," he said to Quinn. "Won't they wait until after your honeymoon? Expenses paid."

"That's your idea of a honeymoon?" Quinn said to Wolfe. "Covering the Yankees on the road?"

"Isn't it wonderful?" she said with a blissful sigh.

"Guess who I ran into in Paris," said Quinn as they buckled themselves into their seats on the Boston shuttle.

"What were you doing in Paris?"

"Killing time before my flight to New York. Nervous?" he said, squeezing her hand.

"I'm much better than I was the last time we flew together. Just don't let go. Who did you see in Paris?"

"The last time we flew together I kissed you. Shall I kiss you again? Would it take your mind off the flight?"

"Kissing you takes my mind off everything, except kissing you."

It was not easy to do, constrained as they were by their seat belts, but they managed it. Quinn kissed her so well and so long she never realized they were airborne until the stewardess interrupted them.

"Excuse me, miss," said the stewardess. "But is this man attacking you?"

"N-n-nooo," mumbled Rainey. "He's suffering from jet lag, and I'm giving him mouth-to-mouth resuscitation."

"Well, it sure looked like he was attacking you." Still disbelieving, she scurried up the aisle.

"You haven't told me who you ran into in Paris."

"Aleksey Kuprin."

"You're kidding. The last time I read about him he was dancing a guest solo with a company in Carson City, Nevada."

"He told me no one in North America understands his style. He has decided to move to France."

"While we are on the subject of moving," she said. "When we get back...don't you think we should start looking for a bigger apartment?"

"I've thought about that . . ."

"Someplace nearer the park . . ." she said.

"If we rented the apartment across the hall, I could break through the kitchen wall and combine them. Dino says . . ."

"Through the wall? That's impossible. You can't go through that wall. I just had it redone. And—"

"But think of the room we'd have."

"That's where the python lives. I couldn't take his home. I'd never forgive you if you and Dino cooked up some scheme to get rid of that guy just because he keeps a snake."

"You've got it all wrong. Dino told me he's planning to move."

"But Quinn, don't you want our kids to be able to play in the park . . ."

"Oh, Rainey," he said, his eyes suddenly huge.

THE YANKEES beat the Red Sox 5-4, and she and Quinn were sharing a cab back to the hotel with two other sportswriters. Three of them crowded into the back seat. With a sly smile Quinn casually dropped his jacket across his lap and half of hers. Beneath it his big hand closed over her thigh. Her leg trembled, and she felt her secret places flutter in anticipation. A silent, smiling Quinn stared out the window while she, for form's sake, tried to join in the banter of the others, trading stories of Yankee-Red Sox contests in the fabled days of Ted Williams. Two can play at this game, she thought, and she slid her hand beneath the jacket. His thigh was as hard as granite and as hot as lava. The cab ride seemed to last forever.

Once inside their room he crushed her in his arms. "I love you, Rainey. I love you so much," he muttered, his voice a harsh rasping whisper. He pressed her against the door, capturing her mouth, teasing her tongue with his own. His breath scalded her throat when he tore his lips away. "I've waited...so long...for this." He spoke in short bursts, panting for breath as he opened her blouse and freed her breasts to his eager hands, and his need inflamed her desire.

Waves of fire broke over her as she tore open his shirt, pressing her breasts against the coarse hair on his chest. He growled with pleasure as her nipples rose hard, and she tangled her hands in his hair. "So have I, my love," she whispered at last. "Oh, so have I."

His clever fingers found the back of her skirt and then she stood flushed and naked in his arms, the rhythm of her eager blood pounding in her ears as he pressed her hard against the door. He outlined her lips with the tip of his tongue, teasing, teasing, teasing— then he conquered them. Her hips moved sinuously against him, and then their bodies locked together so fiercely an image of raging tigers flashed through her mind. Heat poured off him as he entered her, he blazed into her, and she felt so hotly liquid she was sure she could dissolve into him, pass right through the pores of his skin and into the hard burning center that was his core.

On the hot red wall of her mind she saw the picture of the door that opened onto the sky, the sky as blue as forever. She clung to him with all her strength and together they soared beyond the passionate moment, through the doorway and into the hot blue sky.

She must have lost consciousness, because the next thing she knew they were in bed, and she was snuggled against him, her head resting on his shoulder.

"It has just occurred to me," she said, "that we won't be able to do this when you start your editorial job."

"Do what? Make love?" His chest rose and fell with measured slowness.

She pressed her ear to his ribs. It sounded like an airplane hangar in there. "No, silly. Go on the road together with the Yanks. It's time I looked ahead, Quinn. Planned for the future. What would you say if I told you I think I want to be the first woman sports editor of a major metropolitan daily?"

He rubbed his chin against the top of her head. "I'd say, go for it." He slid down in the bed until his mouth touched hers. "That's why I love you. Because you're—"

"Tough as an alligator's knees?"

"Because you're not afraid to take risks, you're not afraid to dream. Because you're your own woman."

"I'm your woman, too, you know."

"Hmmm, do I know that." He kissed her for a long slow time, and then he said, "Rainey, we've never talked about this name thing—whether you want to take my name and be Mrs. Quinn and not Rainey Archer, or whether you want to be known as Rainey Archer professionally and Mrs. Quinn at home."

"We've hardly had time, my darling . . ."

"I think we should make a decision on this before the ceremony."

"I honestly haven't given it a moment's thought," she said. "Have you?"

"All the way back from Paris I kept hearing it in my head."

"Hearing what in your head, my love."

"Rainey Archer-Quinn. Rainey Archer-Quinn. I mean, why should you give up your identity? Why not hyphenate our names? Doesn't Rainey Archer-Quinn have a nice ring to it?"

"Yes, it has a wonderful ring to it. It will look terrific in print, too." She nibbled on his chin. "I am madly in love with your chin, Mr. Quinn. It occurs to me that it's entirely possible that ours could be the first kid with a hyphenated name to play for the Yankees."

"She might at that," said Quinn.

IT WAS OVER BREAKFAST in bed the next morning that Quinn said, "It's a damn shame that old jacket of mine got lost in the mails."

Rainey spread strawberry jam on her toast. "Don't worry about it, darling. We'll get you an even nicer one when we get back to New York. We'll go to Barneys." She munched her toast.

"It's not the jacket," he said. "It's the ring."

She bit her tongue. "Wha wing?"

"I left it in the inside breast pocket. I bought you a wedding band—from Ocean, that ditsy goldsmith in SoHo. Solid. Eighteen carat. Rainey, are those tears in your eyes?"

"I bit my tongue. Darling . . . dearest . . . would you love me no matter what?"

"What do you mean, no matter what? Of course I'd love you no matter what. What kind of question is that?"

"About that wall . . ."

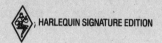
CAROLE MORTIMER

JUST ONE NIGHT

Hawk Sinclair—Texas millionaire and owner of the exclusive Sinclair hotels, determined to protect his son's inheritance. Leonie Spencer—desperate to protect her sister's happiness.

They were together for just one night.
The night their daughter was conceived.

Blackmail, kidnapping and attempted murder add suspense to passion in this exciting bestseller.

The success story of Carole Mortimer continues with *Just One Night*, a captivating romance from the author of the bestselling novels, *Gypsy* and *Merlyn's Magic*.

**Available in March
wherever paperbacks are sold.**

Harlequin Temptation

COMING NEXT MONTH

ATTRACTIVE, SPACE SAVING BOOK RACK

Display your most prized novels on this handsome and sturdy book rack. The hand-rubbed walnut finish will blend into your library decor with quiet elegance, providing a practical organizer for your favorite hard-or soft-covered books.

Only $9.95

Approximately 16" x 8" when assembled

Assembles in seconds!

To order, rush your name, address and zip code, along with a check or money order for $10.70* ($9.95 plus 75¢ postage and handling) payable to *Harlequin Reader Service*:

Harlequin Reader Service
Book Rack Offer
901 Fuhrmann Blvd.
P.O. Box 1396
Buffalo, NY 14269-1396

Offer not available in Canada.

BKR-1A

*New York and Iowa residents add appropriate sales tax.